A KAHALE AND CLAUDE MYSTERY

BOOK 2:

SHADOWS OF DOUBT

TIMOTHY R. BALDWIN

Indies United Publishing House, LLC

First Edition published May 2020

ISBN-13: 978-1-64456-123-2 (paperback)
ISBN-13: 978-1-64456-125-6 (ePub)
ISBN-13: 978-1-64456-124-9 (Mobi)

Library of Congress Control Number: 2020935300

www.indiesunited.net

Also by Timothy R. Baldwin

Bloodshot (2019)

A Kahale and Claude Mystery Series
Book 1: Camp Lenape (2019)
Book 2: Shadows of Doubt (2020)

For my students, past and present.

Chapter One

Marcus

"Runners, take your places," the announcer called through the PA system. Then, the endless drone of the meet rules began. I'd heard it a thousand times before.

Shadows of Doubt

Shoes snug and muscles fully stretched, I strode toward the starting line to join my team and made sure my legs stayed limber. As I did this, I glanced at the cheering fans. Mom and my younger sister Bri waved, but I didn't see Dad. Not immediately, anyway. After a quick scan, I spotted him to the right of the stands. He seemed engaged in an intense conversation with Principal Moss. I knew Moss was no joke when it came to administrating the school. Some would even say he micromanaged everything and everyone at the school, including the students. I guess that was his job. Still, Dad was the school's athletic director. He didn't need Moss on him all the time. Dad was already overworked as he managed over twenty-five sports that regularly made it to the playoffs. Moss needed to let up for just a bit, so Dad could watch my first meet of the season.

"Timers, are you ready?" The announcer asked, which snapped me into focus.

We cheered. I knelt into position. Focusing on the run ahead helped me push the scene between Dad and Moss from my mind.

"Starters, are you ready?" asked the announcer. The announcer paused. "Runners, are you ready?"

In another instance, came a sharp pop. We were off. My legs took control, and my heart seemed to pump fresh blood into my veins. For the moment, my thoughts felt left behind at the starting line. Though Dad wasn't watching, my coach was.

I paced myself, keeping twenty strides behind my rival, another junior named Brad. He played for the Buccaneers of Patterson High and he had no clue he was about to be whooped on the track. This year I planned to take the lead in varsity. I only wished Dad was here, sharing this moment with me.

* * *

"Great job out there today," Mom said.

"Thanks," I said as I breathed heavily.

I looked to Bri, who still hung by the bleachers, with her nose in her cell phone. I just hoped she'd managed to film the end of the meet on her phone. Around the end of the race, I had kicked it into high gear on the track. The roar of the fans still rang in my ears, and the image of Brad, slowing down seconds before the finish line, still lingered in my mind. I had breezed past him to win it all.

I smirked. Hopefully, Dad saw what happened. I looked around, but only adoring parents, doting on their kids, were here.

"Where's Dad?" I asked.

"I'm sorry, honey," Mom said sadly. "Dad had something Principal Moss wanted him to attend to."

I shrugged, but my mood dampened slightly. "No biggie." Before I could figure out where Dad went, Nate Wilson, my best friend, approached. Beside him, came Janice Kane. She was his girlfriend, our fellow classmate, and Alissa Claude's best friend.

"Hey, Mrs. Kahale," Nate and Janice said in unison. They both waved to my mom.

Mom chatted with Janice and Nate. As activities committee chair on the PTSA, Mom wanted to know everything that happened at school.

"How's the drama production coming together?" she asked.

"Fabulous," Janice said.

"Easy for you to say," Nate said as he huffed. "I'm working like a dog backstage."

Once all the pleasantries were done, I looked around. There was no sign of Alissa. "Janice, where's Alissa?" I asked. "Her game should've been over already."

"You know, Marc," Janice said, "there is a thing called a cell phone."

My face grew hot. "I just —"

"Kidding," Janice said with a smile and a twinkle in her eye. "You really do take things literally. She's running late. Check your messages."

When my phone turned on, I caught a quick text from Alissa.

Alissa: *In overtime. Running late. Cya. Hugs.*

I blushed. Alissa and I were also a thing and we grew up together. Getting to the first kiss was, well, more than a little awkward, but maybe I was overthinking it. I hoped we'd get to kiss when our families went to the beach for the upcoming Labor Day weekend.

Nate socked me lightly in the arm, which made me jump.

"Are you okay?" he asked jokingly.

"I'm good, yeah," I said. "Alissa's in overtime."

"Told ya," Janice said. "You're gonna have to get a move on, though. She'll be here soon. I'll meet you guys at the parking lot after Marcus gets cleaned up, okay?"

Nate and I parted ways with Janice and Mom. Bri was still on the bleachers. She stood, raised her arm, and took a duck face selfie on her phone. Then, she bounded down the bleachers to join Mom. I shook my head. My one shred of hope that Bri had video evidence of my victory today disappeared. She could make any moment into a photo op for her vast following on Instagram.

* * *

As we headed to the locker room, we passed the flimsy ticket collection booth. The booth was a shed with faded cream paint that usually got repainted before the season started each year. Dad said it would be replaced with a permanent structure over the summer before the ticketed sports season began. But the renovation still hadn't happened.

"Check that out," Nate said. He glanced behind us.

"That's weird," I said. I looked and saw the doors were open. "Dad always keeps this area locked, even when there's nothing inside. Let's check this out."

As I approached, I saw the lock had been broken. A piece of it was lying in the grass. More disturbing, cabinet drawers and their contents had been tossed about the floors.

"Looks like a break in," Nate offered.

"I don't know why," I said. "There couldn't have been anything valuable inside."

Nate reached in his pocket. "What about game tickets?"

I shook my head. "He keeps those in his office. Do you think this is what Moss was worked up about?"

"Probably." He pulled out a pen and handed it to me. "Here, I'll keep watch from outside."

I gripped the pen. "What's this for?"

As I felt the weight of aluminum in my hand, I noticed the pen point. I clicked the button, which turned on a flashlight. Now, I realized Nate had handed me a tactical pen.

Someone must have stepped up their gadgets, I thought. I set my bag down and entered the shed; its interior illuminated by the glow of the flashlight.

As I searched the room, I saw nothing but tissue boxes, notebooks, and a few old ledgers strewn across the floor. If there was anything valuable in here, which I doubted, it was gone now.

"Marcus," Nate whispered. "We've got to get a move on. Security's coming."

Exiting the booth, I saw Nate already had my bag over his shoulder. A hundred yards away, two security guards ran towards us, closing the distance too quick for my comfort.

Together, we jogged toward the parking lot. Security shouted at us to come back. But we ignored them, hoping they didn't catch a glimpse of us. No way I wanted to answer for a crime I didn't commit.

Our feet hit the parking lot, where I spotted Nate's Jeep. Janice stood in the front seat, her arms flailing as we ran faster to reach her. "Hurry up, you two!" She shouted.

I hopped in the back of the Jeep, while Nate keyed the ignition. He peeled out of the parking lot before Janice or I could even buckle-up.

Chapter Two

Alissa

I stood in the middle of the bus, leading my soccer team in a celebratory chant as we pulled into the driveway. Suddenly, Nate's Jeep squealed past us. My eyes grew wide as I recognized Marcus, sitting in the backseat, dressed in his cross-country uniform. He clung to the handrail as the Jeep made a sharp turn. Marcus shifted suddenly in his seat, barely able to keep himself from falling out. In the front, Janice, red in the face, shouted something at Nate, who didn't appear to be slowing down.

With my teammates still chanting, I glanced at my phone, wondering whether my friends got my text. It did go through, and they were supposed to wait for me. We planned to go to Slices on the Avenue together.

The bus screeched to a halt and I sat down. From the front, Coach Becky stood up, saying, "All right, girls. Nice playing out there again. I can't say it enough. You run a tight, cohesive squad. Let's recognize our MVPs for today."

I clapped and cheered, only half paying attention to Coach Becky's commendations to the team. As she began to rattle off commendations, the way my friends peeled out of the parking lot reminded me of the past summer. Nate and Marcus together almost always got themselves into trouble. But, at summer camp, Bri went missing, and Nate's and Marcus' little game of detective got real. Something was up with my friends. I knew that much, but I also planned to let Marcus squirm a little bit in his explanation.

I only hoped I could catch up with them for dinner on time so we could catch a movie together. Sort of an informal double date. I checked my phone. I thought for sure Janice would have responded on behalf of the others. Though I shouldn't have been surprised. Like Marcus, she was clinging to her own handrail when they sped out of the parking lot.

"Now, I've got some bad news," Coach Becky continued. "On our way here, I received an email from the school finance office. There's been a delay with our new uniforms."

"No way!" Someone shouted above the grumbles and murmurs. "We've got to wear these itchy-old things again?" This was followed by more grumbles and complaints.

What gives? I thought, wondering if this had anything to do with the proposed budget cuts. Two weeks ago, the school staff had told us we had to wait on uniforms, but promised they'd be in. I tugged at my jersey collar as I stood up again, ready to speak my mind.

"I'm sorry, girls," Coach Becky said. "I really can't say. Something to do with processing our orders."

"Aren't the orders already in?" I asked. "We need them to play against our rivals the Buccaneers next week. We barely made it to the state playoffs last year against them."

Coach Becky gave me a quick glance before she turned her attention to the rest of the team.

"Crisp new uniforms don't make the team," she said, adding an intentional pause. "Those who practice hard and play harder make the team. On three for beating the Buccaneers... One, two, three."

We all cheered and began to file out of the bus, slapping high fives with Coach Becky as we did so. I knew what she was doing. She was right; the uniforms don't make the team. But I wasn't going to be fooled either.

"Hey, coach," I said after she high-fived me. "We're going to have the uniforms next week, right?"

"Alissa," Coach Becky said. "I didn't say that. I can only promise they're on order, okay?"

I nodded. "These uniforms are ancient. I just don't want the Buccaneer girls making fun of us again."

Coach Becky sighed. "I get it. I wore those when I went to school here, and they were old then. I'll try my best."

I smiled weakly. I respected Coach Becky. I got the feeling she either had no idea when the order was coming. Or someone forgot to put the order in. I decided I'd let it go for more pressing matters. Checking my phone, I saw I'd gotten a couple of text.

Janice: *Really sorry. Didn't mean to ditch. The boys caught some trouble.*

Marcus: *Will explain what happened. Will make it up to you tonight. Can't wait to see you.*

I grinned and texted Marcus back. *I can't wait to see what you have planned.*

As I headed to the girls' locker room to clean up, there was a bounce in my step. The idea of wearing itchy old uniforms for another game or two sucked. Still, I looked forward to letting Marcus squirm a little throughout the night as he tried to "make it up to me" tonight.

* * *

A bell chimed as I stepped into Slices at the Avenue, located directly across the movie theatre. Marcus stood as I entered. Janice and Nate turned and waved but remained in their seats. Sheepishly, Marcus approached.

"Alissa," he said. "I... uh... you look really pr— beautiful tonight."

I crossed my arms. "You have to do better than that."

Blushing, Marcus looked around, as if looking for support.

Gently slapping his arm, I said, "I'm just kidding. Are you okay? It seems like you all had a tough time getting over here."

Marcus cocked his head. "You saw all that?"

"Yup!" I said, hooking my arm into his and leading us to the booth. "Now, you've got some explaining to do." When we slid in the bench across from Janice and Nate, I added, "All of you, I mean." I leaned in. "Because whatever it was has got to be crazy for you all to leave me hanging at once."

As Marcus began to fill me in on what he saw, Nate thoughtfully scratched the stubble of his chin. Ultimately, what Marcus and Nate filled me in on was so underwhelming that Janice had to add dramatic effect at the end.

"Oh my gosh, Lis," she beamed. "You would've thought they were being chased by a wild boar the way the two of them ran. Then, Nate almost killed us both when we nearly slipped out of our seats as we passed the team bus."

Matching Janice's own enthusiasm, I forced a squeal, "That's totally nuts." I paused and dropped it down a notch. "But I'm glad you're all okay. You think security recognized you?"

"When he first saw us, probably not," Marcus said. "But the way Nate drives and the fact that he's the only one with a Jeep at school, probably."

Nate shrunk in his seat. "Didn't think about that. But there was this guy in the back seat screaming at me to get out of there."

I laughed, nudging closer to Marcus. "Now what?"

Marcus, putting a friendly arm around my shoulder, said, "I'll let Dad know about what we saw when I see him tonight."

"That reminds me," I said. "There's a hold up with our new uniforms. Can you ask your dad about that tonight?"

"Yeah, definitely," Marcus said. "I wonder what the deal is. Dad's usually pretty quick on getting new equipment for the teams."

As we hung out for another half hour before the movie, Janice cuddled up next to Nate. She'd pull globs of cheese off her pizza and plop it on Nate's plate. He'd gobble it up while she made a face and laughed, commenting on how gross cheese is. We gave up on telling her to order a tomato pie instead.

Yeah, they're a weird pair with surprisingly ingenious approaches to life at times. Not that giving away unwanted cheese to someone more than willing to kill it in one bite is ingenious. But it is complimentary. They suit each other.

Just like Marcus and I... well, we've known each forever, but we're still figuring out this couple's thing.

Chapter Three

Marcus

That night, the muggy night air clung to me in sweaty discomfort as Alissa and I got out on either side of the backseat of Nate's Jeep. Earlier, he'd put the top on because of the rain.

On the passenger side of the Jeep, Alissa and Janice engaged in animated conversation. On the driver's side, Nate and I fist-bumped.

"You two going to hang-out for a bit?" Nate asked.

I ran a hand through my hair as I stole a glance at Alissa. Her smiling eyes met my own. Then, she turned back to Janice.

"Yeah, we're about to chill," I said, though I hoped Nate and Janice would be leaving soon.

"Good times," Nate said.

Standing there, I thought of Alissa and me hanging out much later than we should. I shivered. The A/C was still blasting in the Jeep even though the windows were wide open.

Janice laughed. "Okay, Lis! Kisses. You two have fun at the beach this weekend."

Nate's eyes widened as he looked at me. "Last truly free weekend before our junior year is in full swing. Live it up, kids!"

"Thanks, bro," I said. "See you, Tuesday."

Alissa joined me on the sidewalk. We waved to Nate and Janice as they took off, then she turned to me. Though she wore her braids in an updo tonight, she still brushed a hand over her ear as if to adjust a stray braid. Beneath the single streetlamp on our block, her dark brown eyes twinkled.

"Some, night, huh?" she said with a chuckle.

I grinned, thinking about Nate and Janice. They were all over each during dinner and didn't really stop until the end of the movie.

"Maybe we skip the double dating with them next time," I offered.

"Totally," Alissa agreed. "I don't think I can take another meal with them ogling each other."

We both laughed. Though Janice and Nate were our best friends and officially dating only a few days before us, they'd gotten super physical, super-fast. It was beginning to make me feel uncomfortable, and I could tell by the way Alissa had shifted closer to me during dinner, she felt the same. But we weren't about to tell them that.

We turned toward our houses sitting side-by-side with an open front lawn. Our backyards were divided by a chain-link fence down the alleyway. Alissa and I grew up together, first as little kids cautiously staring at each other through that fence. As we got older, we'd playfully tease each other until we were inseparable and finishing each other's sentences. We'd been in the friendship groove for years. But I felt like little kids again. Maybe we were just having a hard time transitioning from being best friends to being a couple. I was probably just overthinking it.

"Care to share your thoughts?" Alissa asked.

"Am I that obvious?" I asked, turning and taking a step toward her.

She looked up at me and smiled. "We've been standing here saying nothing for a minute."

I grabbed her hand. "Just enjoying the moment with you."

Alissa chuckled and placed a hand on my chest. "You're such a bad liar."

In the silence, we gazed at each other. Leaning toward me, Alissa tilted her head and parted her lips. I took the invitation and returned the gesture. There was a slight tremble in her hand, or maybe those were my hands trembling in hers. The last time we tried this, I'd missed and gotten the side of her mouth while bumping our noses together.

Alissa lowered her head. That was it — I'd waited too long; the moment was gone and replaced by massive disappointment.

"Are you guys going to kiss, or what?" asked a familiar, annoying voice that seemed to pierce through the night.

We turned. Alissa stifled a laugh.

"So not cool, Bri," I said.

Bri stood up from the stoop. Her thick, dark curls seemed lopsided, and she wore her pink summer pajamas.

"Why aren't you in bed?" I asked.

Bri crossed her arms as she came over to us. "I could ask you two the same thing?"

"Touché," I said with sarcasm.

"Seriously, why are you up so late?" Alissa asked.

Bri took a deep breath. "Mom and Dad were arguing."

"About what?" I asked a little too loudly. I lowered my voice when I heard it echo through the neighborhood. "When did this happen?"

Bri shrugged. I looked at Alissa. She bit her lower lip.

"Don't worry about the weekend," she said. "I'd understand if..." her voice trailed off.

"No," I said. "We're going. I'm pretty sure it's already paid for."

Alissa nodded, hugging herself as though she was cold.

The front door of our house opened, and Dad stepped onto the porch. He didn't carry the usual coach swagger. Instead, there was a sag in his shoulders. He gripped the railing as he stepped off the porch and stumbled once on the walkway as he came over to us.

"Marcus," Dad said. "Your mom and I need to talk to you inside." He glanced at Alissa as if noticing her for the first time. He forced a smile. "Hope you guys had a good time tonight. Alissa, tell your father I say, 'hi,' okay?"

Marcus

Alissa took her cue to leave as Dad walked back toward the house. Before Alissa left, she gave me a quick side-hug and whispered. "Don't forget to tell him about the ticket booth."

She pulled away. I held her hand, wishing she'd stay. "I'll work it into the conversation. That and the thing with your soccer uniforms."

"Alright," she said, giving me a squeeze. "I'll be up if you want to talk."

"So," Bri said. "If you guys are done. Mom and Dad are waiting."

Bri turned toward the house, and I followed as Alissa made her way next door.

* * *

When I stepped inside, Bri turned to me and whispered, "I don't know what they were arguing about, but it sounded like a big deal. So... good luck."

As she bounded up the steps, my heart sank. Somehow, I expected all this fuss would include my sister and me. I turned into the living room where Dad was slouching on the couch. Several empty beer cans sat on the coffee table in front of him. He held one in his hand. The sight was surreal, like I stepped into an alternate universe. As the athletic director at Lenape High, Dad's big on healthy eating and fitness. He just doesn't drink. At least, not that I'd seen before this moment.

Waiting, I stood in the middle of the living room. Dad stared at a blank TV screen and took another swig, seemingly unaware of my presence. As I shift my weight from one foot to the next, I wondered whether Mom would be joining us, or if it was just going to be Dad and me. He clanked an empty can onto the coffee table, startling me.

"I'm sorry about today," Dad said. "Principal Moss had to pull me away on some urgent matter." He looked at me and forced a sad smile. "Sit down, tell me how it went."

"First place," I said. "But there was this other runner who we have to watch out for in the future. We were neck-to-neck almost to the end, and —"

"That's great, son," Dad interrupted me as he cracked open another beer can.

I stared at him as he seemed to gulp half of it down. "Anyway, maybe you'll be there next time."

"Maybe," he said.

"I think Bri recorded the whole thing," I added, hoping to continue the conversation. When Dad didn't say anything, I was starting to think that maybe I was talking to some imposter version of him. A strange sense of intruding on

Dad's space invaded me. The area on the couch between myself and Dad might as well have been a mile-wide chasm.

"Got something on your mind?" Dad asked.

I wanted to say, *In fact, I have plenty on my mind.* But I didn't. Instead, I thought about how Moss had been yelling at him earlier. Totally out of character for Moss and, in my opinion, uncalled for. That had to be the reason for the momentary distance between Dad and me.

"You and Moss," I said. "Is everything okay?"

Wide-eyed, Dad shot a glance at me. "I didn't know you saw that," he said. "It's nothing for you to worry about, though. I'm handling it."

I nodded, feeling helpless. "As we were leaving, Nate and I noticed the ticket booth looked like someone broke into it."

Dad stiffened up. "Did you see who did it?"

"No," I said. "It was already broken into. I should've gotten pictures, but my phone was in my bag. So, we went in to check it out."

He set down his beer and turned toward me, suddenly giving me his full attention. As he leaned in, I caught a whiff of his sour breath.

"What did you see?" he asked with urgency. "Was anything taken?"

I shifted away. "Not that I could tell. There wasn't a football game today, so I figured there wasn't much to take. Some pens and papers had been thrown about the room. That's it."

"What about the cabinets?"

I ran my fingers through my hair. "They were open."

Dad's jaw went to work like he was chewing on a piece of tin. He sunk back into the sofa cushion and stared at the television. A motion picture, visible only to himself, must've been playing in his mind. Like the TV, Dad was off. Needing to get out of there, I stood and grabbed my duffel bag off the floor.

"Don't worry about any of that," Dad said at last. "I'll clear this up with Moss in the morning."

"Dad, can I ask you about something else?" I asked.

He looked up. "Go ahead. You know you can ask me anything."

"Alissa mentioned her team's uniforms hadn't come in," I said.

Dad frowned. "That purchase should've gone through already. I'll ask about that tomorrow as well."

I grinned. "Thanks, Dad. Good night."

As I headed upstairs, I heard the pop and fizz of Dad opening another can. Passing my parents' room on the way to my bedroom, I heard crying. I gave the door a soft knock.

"Come in," Mom said, her voice cracking as she spoke.

I opened the door. Mom sat on the bed with a box of tissues in her lap. Quickly, she grabbed a wad of tissues sitting by her side and stuffed them out of view.

"Mom, what's going on?" I asked.

"It's nothing, baby," Mom said. She sniffed. "Nothing your dad and I can't handle."

After Dad's evasive remarks, I needed to ask a straight question and get a straight answer. "Are you two thinking about a divorce?"

"Where'd you get that idea?" Mom placed her head in her hands.

I shrugged. "Just needed to ask."

"Oh, Marcus." She stood and embraced me while planting a kiss on my forehead. "I promise you. It's not a divorce."

"Then what?" I asked, holding her gaze.

She sighed. "Just some money problems."

I frowned. "Are we canceling the trip this weekend? We can if—"

"Don't worry about that," Mom said, cutting me off. She gave me a tight smile. "We'll be fine, I promise."

I kissed Mom goodnight and headed past Bri's room, wondering if she heard the whole thing. I didn't bother to check in on her. If anything, Bri probably had her earbuds stuffed in her ears while endlessly watched YouTube, or "hanging out" with her friends through the hottest social media app. As if on cue, I heard her laughter on the other side of the door.

Like I thought, Bri was fine. Though, I wasn't so confident about myself or the rest of my family.

* * *

That night I struggled to fall asleep as one thought after another bombarded my brain. Dad was definitely off. He couldn't keep his thoughts straight in the same way he couldn't keep himself from stumbling around. It was like someone had smacked him in the head with a two-by-four he hadn't seen coming. Then Mom's evasive and moderately satisfying answer to my question of divorce. If not divorce, then why had she been crying? No way she'd be wasting tears over a little money problem. It had to be about so much more than a few bucks.

My phone chimed. I grabbed it.

Alissa: *You okay?*

Me: *Yeah. Mom and Dad aren't.*

Animated dots popped up on my screen. I wondered if Alissa's parents knew what was going on. My parents and hers were really close.

Alissa: *What happened?*

Me: *No idea. Mom says money problems.*

Alissa: *WTF. That's insane.*

I thought about telling her about Dad's drinking and Mom's crying, but I thought better of it.

Me: *Yeah. But we're still on for the beach.*

Alissa: *ikr? Can't wait to spend the weekend with you.*

Me: *Me too.*

After I sent my text, I added a kiss emoji. Animated dots appeared on my screen. My heart thudded in my chest. A part of me wished I hadn't sent that emoji. The animated dots seemed to go on forever. I put my phone down.

It buzzed.

The first thing I noticed was the kiss emoji Alissa sent back to me.

Alissa: *Love you lots.*

Me: *Love you lots, too. Cya in the morning.*

I laid back down and stared into the darkness, wondering if that was the right response. Well, it was better than not responding. Alissa wouldn't let me hear the end of it if I didn't, especially with a long weekend ahead. I needed to get away. I just hoped the weekend wouldn't be overshadowed by Mom crying about money issues and Dad suddenly drinking.

Chapter Four

Alissa

A few days later and Marcus and I stood waist-deep in ocean waters. We had found a sandbar to hang out on fifty yards from shore. It was Saturday, and whatever had been going on the other night, seemed to have died down. Or, no one seemed to be showing any interest in talking about it. Certainly not Marcus, who appeared to be handling whatever it was pretty well. But, like the ocean waters, I knew things could change in an instant.

Suddenly, I found myself gagging and spitting out salt-water as a wave splashed against my face.

Marcus laughed. "You're not supposed to drink it."

Like a shark, I sank beneath the ocean's surface and grabbed Marcus' legs, lifted him, and flipped him over. When I rose, I couldn't see him, but I knew he was there, lurking just below the surface. His hands brushed against my leg. I screeched even though I knew it was him. I backed away. When Marcus bobbed back up, his back was to me. I took advantage of the moment by jumping on him, bringing us both below the surface again. I could've done this all day, just Marcus and me.

"Hey," Marcus said after we rose again. "The water's getting rough. We should go in."

As I looked out across the ocean, I could see the waves getting choppier. Somehow, I'd missed the signs, or maybe I just ignored them. The wind was picking up, and the sky was beginning to get dark.

"Race ya to the beach," I said.

Before Marcus could respond, I swam toward the shore. Though we were only thirty yards away, the undercurrent was much worse getting back than I expected. I had to fight from keeping it from pulling me under.

* * *

When I finally made it to shore, my toes hugged the sand, still warm and capable of providing relief for my struggles. But I couldn't enjoy it for too long as I swiveled, searching for Marcus. Though he wasn't as strong of a swimmer, he should've been right behind me. Past summers at the beach would have proven otherwise. I stepped toward the water's edge. The remnants of tiny waves crashed against my legs, but I couldn't see Marcus. Without another thought, I ran back into the water until I was waist-deep, though only a few yards from shore. That's when I saw his head bob out of the water.

I called out to him, "Swim parallel to the shore!"

At first, he didn't seem to hear me. I fought every instinct to rush out there and help him. But then he turned his course. His arms let loose long powerful strokes, but he didn't seem to be making any progress. Suddenly, he stopped and allowed himself to bob.

"What are you doing?" I called out to him. I imagined he'd suddenly go under, but he didn't seem to be struggling to stay above water. Quite the opposite, actually. He seemed to be coming closer to me. A moment passed while he remained above water until he swam toward me, this time with much less effort.

When Marcus was close enough, I closed the gap and embraced him. He gasped for breath.

"I thought I'd lost you!" I cried.

"That... was... nuts," Marcus said.

I helped him to the shore where he sat down. Sitting down next to him, I listened to his breath slow to a steady pace. He leaned toward me and kissed my forehead.

"Thank you," he said.

I looked at him. "For what?"

"For being there," he said. A smile tugged at his cheeks. "I'm glad you didn't come in to save me."

"Why'd you stop swimming?"

He sat up and shrugged. "I couldn't tell where the riptide was pulling. I saw this video online with these guys in Australia. They suggested to just let yourself float. So... I did."

"I'm... glad it worked," I said.

I didn't want to imagine what I would've done if it hadn't. Tears suddenly tugged at the corner of my eyes.

Marcus scooted closer to me and wrapped an arm around me. I sniffed and returned the gesture, leaning my head on his shoulder.

"Hey," he whispered in my ear. "It's about to rain."

"Dag, I was just getting comfortable."

Marcus stood and extended his hand to me. I took it and allowed him to pull me up.

When I stood, he said, "Hold on a sec."

I waited, hoping he intended to finish what he started, though he and the weather definitely didn't help with the mood. He looked at me, smirked, then lowered his head. I rolled my eyes, knowing full well what was coming next. Like a dog, he shook out his shoulder-length hair. I backed away, but not before being doused with half the ocean.

"You're such a butt," I said as I giggled. "C'mon, you." I held out my hand.

Marcus took it, and I pulled his arm around my waist. At times, he was impossibly incorrigible. But we still had the weekend. We walked like that for a hot second before I hip bumped him.

"Hey," he yelped. He stumbled once, then tripped and landed in the sand. "What was that for?"

"I'll tell you if you can catch me." With a devilish grin, I took off in a sprint.

I hoped he couldn't catch me. Marcus' long legs and lanky frame were built for distance, not for the short spurt of speed that soccer had prepared me for. Besides, I definitely put him at a disadvantage when I knocked him off balance.

Marcus slowed down when he closed the distance between us. He was barely out of breath.

"Who's the butt, now?" He asked mischievously.

"Still you," I said, putting distance between us once again.

Tying, we came to the beach house, a cliched blue with the white trim rancher. Outside the house, Bri was gathering up her things. She'd built an impressive three-story sandcastle, complete with moat and drawbridge, all of which would be washed away in the coming storm.

* * *

After helping Bri with her things, we made our final dash to the porch as we were pelted with fat drops of rain. Lightning struck, and thunder cracked as the wind picked up. As we dried off, the rain pelted the roof.

"You guys were just in time," Bri said. "What were you doing out there anyway?"

Marcus blushed. "None of your business."

Bri huffed and looked at me. "Probably not business worth knowing."

She was only half-right.

When we entered the house, I noticed my parents and Marcus' mom hustling about the kitchen as though they were preparing for a super-bowl party. But, Marcus' dad, Mr. Kahale, not so much. He was sitting on the couch with a bottle of beer in his hand. There were two more empties on the floor beside him.

I gave Marcus a glance, but he seemed to avoid my eye-contact.

From the kitchen, my mother waved us in. "Hey, kids. Lunch is almost ready. Why don't you three get changed?"

I nodded. Mr. Kahale didn't seem to notice us at the door. He was staring at the TV. This wouldn't have been unusual; except he wasn't watching sports. The weather channel was on as though he couldn't just take a look outside. I glanced at Marcus. His jaw was clenched.

"Hey, Dad," Marcus said.

Mr. Kahale kept his attention focused on the weather channel. "Looks like you kids got in just in time."

"Yeah," Marcus said. "The waves were pretty intense out there. That's when we got out."

"My sandcastle won't stand a chance," Bri said. She held up her phone, "You wanna see it, Dad?

Bri plopped herself right down beside her dad. She leaned against him as her hair dragged a wet spot across the leather sofa. Flipping through her phone, Bri placed it right in front of him. Mr. Kahale grunted and nodded at each picture.

"That's a great castle," Mr. Kahale said. He didn't even try to feign enthusiasm.

"Diner'll be ready in a few," my mother called. "Get upstairs and change."

It was like she'd read my mind. I was ready to go upstairs and change because this scene was a total drag. Marcus' downcast eyes told me he was getting the same vibe.

Bri kissed her dad on the cheek and popped out of the seat. At least she wasn't letting her dad's dark cloud ruin her afternoon. Marcus and I followed her upstairs.

I couldn't help but think about how Mr. Kahale was so not himself. In the past, he would've gone out to the beach with us. Not only that, but he would've built the sandcastle, tackled Marcus in the water, and bought us salt-water taffy on the boardwalk right before dinner. But today, he didn't seem to do anything. I had a hard time believing he had been in all day watching the weather channel. Not to mention the beer. I mean, three beers are nothing. My father would drink that in a minute. But that I know of, the Kahales have never had liquor in their house. Nor have they ever brought beer to the beach.

* * *

After showering off, I stood in front of the bedroom mirror, using a towel to squeeze the last bit of water out of my hair. A knock came at the door.

"It's open," I called.

Marcus peeked in and grinned. "You look amazing."

I glanced down at my t-shirt. It was pink with blue floral patterns, the color of which matched my shorts and the beach house.

"Thanks," I said and added a hint of sarcasm. "I was going to throw on a shapeless burlap bag, but I didn't want to itch all night."

Marcus stepped inside and sat on the bed. "Yeah... well. You still look amazing."

"You too," I said. My face flushed. Marcus looked cute in a dorky way. His hair hung loosely at his shoulders, and he wore a Hawaiian button-up shirt with khaki cargo shorts. The shorts threw me off.

Alissa

"I have to ask," I said. "When did you start wearing cargo shorts?"

He patted the side-pockets. "You mean *why*."

I cocked my head. "Okay. I'll bite. Why?"

Marcus pulled out a heavy-looking pen. "I've got a couple of things."

"What the heck?" I exclaimed. "You gonna write a note or something?"

He shook his head. "It's a tactical pen. Nate said I should get one. You know, just in case." He shrugged and handed it to me.

The bottom of the pen pointed out into a terrifying-looking metal cone. I rubbed my finger over it. "What this for?" I asked.

"That's the strike point," Marcus said.

I nodded, imagining it would do some severe damage if you hit someone in the right spot. "You planning on using this tonight?"

He shook his head. "I'll bring it with me because you never know."

I nodded and handed it back to him, thinking of a few times when something like this would've come in handy.

Bri peeked in. "You two smooching yet?"

Marcus's shot her a daggered look, which made my face grow hot. Bri was the closest thing I had to a little sister. I loved her to death, but she also annoyed me like a little sister. Before Marcus could chase after her, I did.

Bri skipped down the hall and sang, "Lunch is ready!"

* * *

The evening air was crisp and damp from the storm earlier that day. Marcus and I held hands as we walked the boardwalk and observed the crowds. People shopped the vendors and played carnival games. We walked in silence, sharing in the heaviness of the evening meal that couldn't have ended soon enough.

"Marc," I said. I paused. I wasn't exactly sure how to bring up the problem that was obviously bothering us both.

Marcus stopped and let go of my hand. "Lis... I'm sorry about my dad. He's... I don't know."

"You don't have to apologize," I said. "It's not your fault."

Marcus cringed. "I've never seen him drink." He raked his hands through his hair. "I just don't get it. He wouldn't even sit down for dinner with us."

I waited, not wanting to bring up the totally awkward conversation between his dad and mine. Marcus turned away from me. I realized he was on the verge of tears.

"Listen," I said. I placed my hands on Marcus' waist and drew close to him. "We'll get through this."

"I know," Marcus said. "It's just..."

I placed my finger to his lips. "Something's really eating him up. It's bothering you, too. You know I'm here for you."

Marcus nodded. "He's drinking at home. We seem to be going broke. I don't know what's going on."

Thinking he had more to tell me, I waited.

The boardwalk's neon lights flickered on, catching a twinkle off Marcus' glistened eyes. Marcus gently took my hand and kissed it. When he flashed me a crooked smile, my face flushed again. Walking hand in hand, I realized we'd shared a moment. One in which we were completely present to each other.

We came to a neon putt-putt golf sign. It had an arrow pointing to a rooftop deck.

"Hey," Marcus said. "You want to play a round of putt-putt. Bet I can beat you this time."

"This time?" I asked. "Babe, I've got a record to keep. C 'mon."

Playfully, we pulled on each other as we ascended some rickety wooden steps until we reached the rooftop deck of the building. The AstroTurf sparkled with light from overhead lamps, and somewhere close by the zap and pop of electricity announced the death of another hapless bug. It was an oddly romantic setting. Or maybe that was my own desire playing tricks on me. I only knew the night was definitely not about me.

Chapter Five

Marcus

Tuesday morning, Bri slammed the car door shut and bounded off toward the front door of her middle school. For once, her cell phone was stuffed in her back pocket as she greeted her friends: Nyah, from summer camp, and a few others I didn't bother to get to know.

As Dad pulled out of the parent drop-off, I envied my little sister. We'd driven in what might as well have been absolute silence from the house to here while Dad spouted off football stats from seasons past. Occasionally, I got a word in about my cross-country career, but as soon as I did, he'd nod, say something about getting a scout out, then move on back to football.

I wasn't sure I could manage another five minutes. "Dad, um, drop me off right here, okay?'

Dad kept driving, ignoring me entirely until he said, "Interesting weekend."

"Yup," I agreed, letting him lead the conversation in one of two imaginable topics: his drinking or my nearly drowning.

"How long have you and Alissa been going together?" He asked.

A momentary pause on my part to get over my surprise. "Since the summer, I guess."

"Have you two..." Dad began, but let his voice trail off, clearly hoping I'd get where he was going with this.

And I did. "Nope," I said. "We haven't even kissed yet."

Eyes blinking rapidly, Dad stared straight ahead. Though, I'm sure he wasn't really watching the road. Twice, maybe three times, he licked his lips as if they were dry.

"Jeez, Dad," I said. "I'm already a little self-conscious about it."

"No, I," Dad sputtered. "I mean... don't worry about it. It'll come. The kissing I mean. You two will know what to do when the time comes. As for... uh... the other thing... well, wait until you're married. Okay?"

"Sure," I said. *The other thing*, as Dad called it, was the furthest thing from my mind.

After another few minutes of silence, we pulled into the parking lot.

"Whelp," Dad said as he parked in his usual spot. "This is it."

Neither one of us took the initiative to open the car door. Dad was due in the building much sooner than I was. As for myself, I could've sat in the car another thirty minutes. But I usually got out at this point and hung with my squad. Dad seemed to be waiting for something.

"Dad," I said. "How's everything going with you and Mom?"

"Aside from the money problems, we're fine," he said. "Listen, I need to make a phone call. Why don't you head in without me this morning?"

"Sure," I said, though there were still other things, like the drinking, that I needed to ask him about. "I'll see you tonight."

He stared at his phone. "Have a great day. Stay out of trouble, okay."

Grabbing my gym bag and my book-bag, I got out without responding to him. He and Mom were telling me everything was fine. But Dad's behavior over the weekend didn't have me fooled. I'm pretty sure it didn't have Mom fooled either.

As I reached for the front door, I took a glance over my shoulder. The faded maroon station wagon remained where I left it. Likewise, Dad remained where I left him. He wasn't on his phone, but he did wave at me.

"Hey," a familiar voice whispered. It took me a second to catch Nate peering from around a pillar near the front door.

"Why are you hiding?" I asked.

"Pretty sure security identified us from our little shed incident," Nate said. "We need a way in without getting spotted."

"What're we going to do?" I asked. "Hang out here and shuffle on in with the crowd?"

Nate shrugged. "Or we could sneak on through the gym entrance. You know, when Alissa and Janice have PE?"

"That's not until the second period," I said. "We'd be marked absent in our first period."

Nate cocked his head and frowned. "We could always claim our first-period teacher somehow missed us."

"I don't think so," I said. "C'mon. Stop fooling around. I'm going inside to study."

"Alright," Nate said as he followed me inside. "But don't say I didn't —"

"Gentlemen," Principal Moss' voice resounded off the linoleum floor and concrete walls. "Glad you could make it, bright and early, no less."

"Dad and I usually get here at this time, so..." I shrugged.

Moss ignored my reply and continued. "Follow me into the office. Security has a few questions for you. I don't think you're in trouble, but they are trying to figure out the timeline of events last week."

We followed Moss in through the front door. As we rounded the corner, I spotted school security standing in the glassed-in main office.

"If you're talking about the ticket booth," Nate said. "It was broken when we got there."

Moss grabbed the handle of the office door. "I understand. Still, let me introduce you to our security team."

While introductions weren't necessary, I shook the hands of our security staff, Mr. Koval and Ms. Carrington.

"Why'd you run from us?" Carrington asked.

"We were running late," I offered.

Koval responded with a laugh. "And that's why you" — he pointed at Nate — "raced right out of the parking lot."

"We were really late," Nate said.

"I'm sorry," I said. "Can we start over?" Receiving simultaneous nods in the affirmative from Koval, Carrington, and Moss, I continued. "We were headed to the parking lot and noticed the door was open. My Dad, Mr. Kahale, keeps it locked. But, upon further inspection, we found the lock was broken and on the ground."

"Then you went inside," Carrington said. "Did you take anything? Destroy anything?"

"Nothing," Nate said. "Even if we wanted to, there wasn't anything to take."

"It was just a bunch of junk," I said. "That's it."

Moss spoke up. "See, I told you two these outstanding young men had nothing to hide." He turned to us. "Would you two mind writing two separate reports detailing what you found?"

Without waiting for our reply, he swiped his radio off the counter and sauntered out the door. As he left, his oversized suit coat seemed to flap behind him like a cape.

"Here you are, boys," Carrington said, handing us each an official-looking piece of paper.

Koval added, "Marcus, sit on over here. And, remember, be as detailed as possible."

Sitting adjacent to each other, Nate and I eyed each other. Neither of us seemed to get a sense of what to write. Then, I guess we just began at the beginning. From there, ideas seemed to flow right out of me. I don't know why, but they seemed to be making a pretty big deal out of an old shed that was going to be replaced anyway. Come to think of it, even Dad had been on the edge of extreme pushiness when I had brought up the vandalism of the shed last week.

Chapter Six

Alissa

The girls' locker room buzzed with life at the top of the second period. We were in the middle of a Girl's Volleyball tournament in P.E. Today, Mr. Kahale, Marcus' dad and our P.E. teacher, promised an updated leaderboard. In the meantime, the girls slung a whole lot of good old-fashioned trash-talk as we changed and filed out to the gym floor.

The shrill shriek of a whistle put an end to all that, though. Especially when we caught sight of a pot-bellied, oddly muscle-bound man with the whistle in his mouth. We all stood there, staring, mouths agape.

"Alright, ladies," the man shouted. "For those of you who don't know, I'm Mr. Dunbar, your substitute while Kahale is out."

Dunbar waited as a wave of whispers spread amongst us.

"What's he talking about?" Janice nudged me. "Did Marcus say anything to you?"

I shook my head. "Haven't seen him yet. But their car was out front when I came in."

Marcus didn't say anything about his dad having the day off. Still, I wondered if it had anything to do with his dad's behavior over the weekend.

"Maybe he took the day off to rest?" I offered. "The beach trip definitely wiped him out."

"Yeah?" Janice asked. "How was it with you and Marcus?"

As Dunbar introduced himself with impossible to fact-check claims about a football career he had going for him in another lifetime, I caught her up.

"Seriously, Lis, I can't believe you didn't kiss," Janice said. "We've got to work on your game."

I rolled my eyes. "Anyway. Marcus didn't say anything about his dad being off today. We texted for a minute last night, but nothing about school."

Out of nowhere, Dunbar shouted, "Everyone needs to stop talking now." Red-faced, he waited. Janice, like so many others in the class, crossed her arms and took a bored, slouching stance. She was irritated, just like the rest of us. Just like me.

"Thank you," Dunbar smiled in a tight-lipped attempt to bottle up his insincerity. "Since Kahale will be out for a while, I thought we'd begin with football."

Protests erupted, with Janice being the loudest in her complaint. "You can't expect us to play football. Look at us, we're —"

"Don't worry," Dunbar said with silk in his voice. "It's flag football, not contact."

I stepped forward. "Mr. Dunbar, sir. We're actually in the volleyball unit. We're in the middle of —"

"Playing football," Dunbar interrupted me, then glanced at his clipboard before looking up and speaking again. "You're Alissa Claude. Right?"

"Yes, sir," I said. "Why?"

With clenched jaw muscle, Dunbar seemed to carefully chew on a new idea before spitting it out. "Excellent," he grinned and tossed his clipboard to the side. "You're team captain."

Not knowing what to say, I stood there listening to snickers behind me. Either someone was playing a trick on me, or Dunbar was targeting me. Either way, I didn't like it.

"Don't look so shocked," Dunbar said. "You're team captain for the soccer team. You're a shoo-in for a simple game of flag football."

I wasn't so sure. Some of my classmates, the ones who are the most athletic, were already starting to stretch. Janice, like the other non-competitives, remained standing there in an even more intentional slouch.

I turned back to Dunbar. "Thanks," I said. "But you've got to understand, Volleyball is —"

"Or you can take second-string on the soccer team," Dunbar said.

I clamped my mouth shut. I was pretty sure Dunbar didn't have that kind of authority. Still, I also wasn't about to test his ability to follow through on this threat.

"Thank you for your cooperation," Dunbar said and pointed. "Take that corner, please."

I trudged on over to the far corner of the gymnasium while he called up three other unfortunate girls: an athlete, a beanpole, and a girl who played flute in the marching band. These he appointed as team captain for the other teams.

One after another, Dunbar pointed at each girl with a *hey you*. Each shuffled their way over to a corner of the gym to join their team captain. By the third round, his obvious social engineering experiment was underway. Literally, on appearances alone, he seemed to determine the athlete from the non-athlete, the competitive from the noncompetitive. Not a single girl assigned to her team looked anything at all like the previous girl. Still, one team was clearly stacked with some of the top athletes, and it wasn't my team. For a hot second, I thought Dunbar might've been clever had it not been his first day as our sub. I wondered if the team assignments would've been different had I not stepped up. Sadly, though, it wasn't. Even sadder, Janice wasn't even on my team.

* * *

The whistle blew perfunctorily. With a shout, Dunbar demanded a ten-minute warm-up — we jogged in place — followed by a full-body stretch, followed by a grueling five minutes of lateral suicides. During this last warm-up, the non-competitives, Janice included, seemed to slow down out of sheer exhaustion or sheer boredom. Not me, though. I could do these exercises in my sleep.

As I passed Janice the second time, I urged her on with, "C'mon, girl! You've got this."

With a roll of her eyes, she trotted lazily along. I didn't blame her. She hardly bought into volleyball.

Still, I had to give credit to Dunbar. He knew Kahale's warm-up routine pretty well. That's where the similarities ended.

The whistle blew, calling us to scrimmage. Two teams took their places on either side of the gymnasium. Once there, we hooked belts over our waists.

"Heads up," Dunbar shouted. He tossed a football, one to each court. Quicker than the others, I caught ours, much to the protests of the other team.

"Alright, ladies," Dunbar shouted. "Each team to their goal lines. Even teams take kickoff."

Sixty of us stared back at him, blinking.

"Mr. Dunbar," Janice said, her voice echoing off the gymnasium walls. "Do we literally kick the ball because—"

Dunbar sighed, "If you want. Or you can throw it. If it's dropped during a kickoff, someone else can pick it up and run it to the end zone." He paused. "You all know what an end zone is?"

No one answered. "Alright, get on it." He blew the whistle.

For the rest of the period, all of us played terribly. Not to our fault, though. Dunbar's whistle repeatedly shrieked, followed by shouted phrases like "Offsides," "Touchback," or "Back to the line of scrimmage."

Literally, in the middle of a play, a girl finally said, "What's a line of scrimmage?"

Dunbar's whistle fell from his mouth. "It's a —"

The bell rang. As a single unit, every girl unclipped her belt and let it drop to the floor. We all made a mad dash to the locker room, leaving Dunbar standing there, shouting for us to come back and clean up. None of us listened because we all knew we were going to be late for our next class.

* * *

"Can you believe that guy," Janice complained.

"I know," another girl said. "Dunbar's impossible. Worst class ever!"

Another girl, while pulling her shirt over her face, said, "We need to get a petition together. No way can I do another day of flag football."

Janice stepped into her skinny jeans and yanked them up. "Apparently, Mr. Kahale is going to be out for a while, so we'll have to deal with Dunbar."

"What? No way! That sucks!" several girls said.

I nudged Janice. "She's just exaggerating. Maybe he's out because he's sick or something."

Suddenly, all eyes were on me as though I was the prophetic voice of the Kahale Family. I felt my face grow hot.

"I'm just saying," I said. "Mr. Kahale will be back before we know it, and Dunbar will just be a bad dream."

"More like a nightmare," Abby Jenkins, a second-year senior, said. "I'm pretty sure my thigh is going to bruise. Look." She flashed me her leg.

"That's okay," I said as I looked away. "I'm not qualified, and you should probably see the nurse. We're already late, and we've gotta go."

I grabbed Janice's hand, and she swiped up her bag. On our way out, we bumped into a herd of freshman girls.

"Watch it!" Janice said.

"Watch yourself," one of the girls said. "Why're you getting out so late?"

"Substitute. Good luck!" Janice said with a smile.

From behind, the girls from my class pushed against Janice and me, forcing us into the hallway.

"Janice, hurry up," I said, pulling her along to our next class.

"God!" Janice said. "I really hate flag football."

"You hate P.E. in general," I said.

"I know," Janice said. "But you know what's worse?"

"Mr. Dunbar for an indefinite period?" I offered.

"Yeah," Janice said. The late bell rang. "And being late to class every other day, too."

"I doubt he bothered to let the office know of his slip up," I said. Fortunately for us, our next class wasn't too far away. Still, I pulled us along as though we were again running suicides in P.E. class.

"Lis," Janice said, bringing us to a complete stop. "Do you know when Marcus' dad is coming back?"

"Relax," I said. "Kahale will be back before we're in P.E. again."

Alissa

I also wondered if this was true. I've lived next to the Kahales and known them all my life, but I didn't know every secret occurring inside their home.

Chapter Seven

Marcus

That afternoon, I plopped myself down across from Nate at lunch.

"I'm going to go see my dad," I said.

"Why?" Nate asked. "What's up? Something to do with Dunbar?"

"You heard?" I asked.

He held up his phone. A stream of text messages from Janice told me she'd caught Nate up to speed. Conversely, my phone contained one text from Alissa: *See me after class.* Last period she gave me the low-down on what she and Janice called "The Dunbar Disaster."

"Can't believe Dad isn't here," I said to Nate. "He drove me to school. He didn't say anything about having a sub today."

Nate raised an eyebrow. "Your dad tells you everything that goes on here?"

I thought about it for a moment. "Actually... Dad talked endlessly about football stats."

"And he'll talk endlessly about tonight's soccer game and tomorrow's track meet," Nate said. "So what?"

I leaned in. "There's something else."

"Oh?" Nate said and leaned in closer. "I can keep a secret."

"I think he was trying to give me the sex talk," I said.

Nate guffawed. "I got that talk when I was in fifth grade."

"You did?" I asked.

Nate nodded. "Listen, parents can pick the weirdest times to have those types of conversations. I wouldn't think too deeply about it."

"You're probably right," I said.

Nate grinned. "Of course, I'm right. Your dad just needed the day off. Dunbar's covered for him before. We all know he's a terrible sub."

I laughed. Last year Dunbar bragged about making MVP for college ball at UCLA. We looked him up. No such record existed.

"Still, Dad didn't even tell me I would need to get my own ride home."

Nate stood and clapped me on the shoulder. "That's because he doesn't need to. He knows you've got friends who'll get you home."

I wasn't buying it. Instead, I stared at my lunch tray and stirred around a lumpy pile of mashed potatoes as if looking for an omen.

"Bro," Nate said. "Let's settle it. We still have ten minutes. Let's hop on down to his office and see what's up."

Grabbing my chicken sandwich, I followed Nate toward the door and dumped the rest of my tray out in the trash. As we headed out of the cafeteria, I took a few dry bites of the sandwich, struggled to swallow it down, and tossed the rest as we rounded the corner of the hallway headed down to the athletic office.

* * *

Marcus

Though Lenape High boasts a ten-year championship streak in eighty percent of its sports, you wouldn't know it from walking down the athletic wing. Dad's office was located at the end of a narrow musty hallway. As we turned down the hall, a fluorescent bulb flickered as if distressed by a glass display case, housing faded trophies of seasons past.

As we got closer to Dad's office, a clanking sound from the weight rooms caused me to breathe easier. Nate, on the other hand, let out a rapid succession of sneezes from all the dust.

"Follow me," I said. "Dad'll be in here. He sometimes works out during this hour." The clanking of the metal grew louder and more spread out. Exhaustion was beginning to set in for the lifter. "That's weird," I said, stopping Nate.

"What's weird?" Nate asked, then sniffed.

"Dad maintains a pretty steady pace in his reps, not like..." I glanced into the window. Nate remained right behind me. With his broad back toward us, a bulky man in gym shorts and a tight t-shirt used the smith machine to do another quick set of squats. At the final three reps, he grunted in his struggle to lift the weight. On the last rep, I thought about going in to spot him, but with one final huff, he managed to finish the rep.

"That's Dunbar, alright," Nate whispered.

As Dunbar turned, Nate and I ducked. "What does this guy think he's doing?" I whispered.

"Getting cozy," Nate said with a smirk. "What is this? His tenth time subbing here?"

"Something like that," I said, and wondered if Dad knew about Dunbar using the equipment. If he did, he'd lecture him about proper lifting techniques and choosing the right amount of weight. "Let's check Dad's office," I said. "Looks like the door is open, so maybe he's in."

As we came near, I caught a glimpse of file boxes and loose papers scattered about the floor. Dad's not the most organized teacher around the building, but I knew he wouldn't have these boxes spread out all over the floor.

"Dude," Nate said. "I don't know what's going on. But your Dad is disorganized, not messy."

"This kind of reminds me of—"

"Can I help you, boys?" asked a guttural, male voice. When we turned, Dunbar's barrel chest and rounded gut greeted us.

"Hi," Nate said. "We were looking for Mr. Kahale. The athletic director." Nate gave me a nudge, as Dunbar glared at Nate, then at me.

"We were supposed to catch up on some make-up work," I added.

Dunbar crossed his arms. "He's not in today."

I frowned.

"Thanks," Nate said before I could respond. With a nod, Nate motioned for us to leave.

I took his cue and followed. As we walked away, I glanced over my shoulder. Dunbar remained standing there. He seemed deep in thought as he rocked on his heels. Maybe he was waiting for us to leave so he could let loose a fart. I heard weightlifting could do that to a guy.

When we'd gotten out of Dunbar's line of sight, I pulled Nate close to the wall and ignored the glances of students and teachers as they passed by us. "Something seriously strange is going on here," I said.

"Tell me about it!" Nate said. "First, the ticket booth, then your dad's office?"

I nodded, wondering if these two incidents were related. I intended to find out as soon as I found Dad.

Chapter Eight

Alissa

When soccer practice let out that afternoon, I didn't see the Kahales' station wagon in the parking lot. Before I bounced, I shot Marcus a text to make sure he still needed a ride.

I looked up when I heard Janice yell, "Lis, you won't believe this." She ran toward me.

"What's the emergency?" I said.

"Wait, I'll tell you! Just let me catch my breath." Janice reached me and collected herself while I tossed my soccer gear in the back seat of my Nissan.

"What has you so worked up?" I asked.

"Our fall production," Janice huffed. "You know, *In the Heights.* We were booked, and everything! But, out of nowhere, the director canceled!"

"That's terrible," I said, giving Janice my full attention. "You worked so hard on that one song."

Janice frowned. "I know. All that time singing Nina's *When You're Home...* but I'm not home. Not with the musical being canceled." A tear escaped the corner of her eye. She sniffed.

I took a deep breath. "Hey, girl. You're going to do something else, right?"

"That's the thing," Janice said. "Last week, she told us the license was submitted. Today, she's suddenly telling us we're going to do a variety show instead. You know, something royalty-free."

I smiled. "Then, you'll still be able to do the song!"

She shook her head. "You don't understand. This is my dream. I need to play that role!"

She was right; I didn't understand. Not the need to take on a role in a play. In fact, most people in our school didn't get Janice and me. On the surface, we had very few shared interests. I played sports while she did drama. But we both had summer camp, church youth group, and national honor society.

I chewed my lip, thinking about how I could help my best friend achieve her dream. "What about Spring? Maybe NHS and the PTSA could work together to raise funds? We could talk to Marcus' mom."

Janice nodded and gave me a slight smile. "Our director did say if we could raise enough money, we might be able to do that."

At that, I realized something. "How's our school suddenly without money? First, the soccer uniforms, now drama production. No way this could be related to the budget cuts!"

"That's what I'm saying!" Janice said. "We spent all last year working our butts off with *Putnam County Spelling Bee*. You saw it. It sold out every night. We even had to add additional performance dates. They weren't as sold out, but still..."

Janice continued talking as I figured, at ten bucks for general seating and half that for student tickets, with a house that seats fifteen hundred people, and six shows.

Alissa

I interrupted Janice's ramblings about theatre. "What'd you guys bring in? Twenty thousand? How much did the show cost?"

Janice blinked. "I... I really don't know. Between the sets and the live orchestra... maybe..." She shrugged as her voice trailed off.

"How about you figure that one out," I said as I spotted Marcus crossing the parking lot toward us.

Janice glanced over her shoulder, then back at me. She placed her hands on her hips, cocked her head, and wiggled her eyebrows. "Oooh. I see what you're up to." She grinned, then dramatically hoisted her right hand into the air. "A case, ladies and gentlemen. We have a case!"

"As long as it doesn't involve basements," I said. I laughed nervously, thinking about our first case at camp this past summer.

"You got that, right," Janice said.

"What's this about a case now?" Marcus asked.

"Just a thing we're talking about," Janice said. "Have you seen Nate?"

Marcus did a quick 360-degree scan of the parking lot as if Nate was about to pop out from behind one of the cars, which wasn't unlikely.

Marcus shook his head. "He was supposed to meet me out here. He was in sixth period class with me. But, at the end of the day, he checked out. Here," Marcus reached into his pocket and handed Janice a phone. "He wanted me to give this to you. I guess you left your phone with him."

Janice suddenly stiffened and her eyes beamed. She grinned sheepishly and grabbed her phone. "Talk to you later!" she yelled. "Bye!"

With a grin, Marcus watched her go. I, on the other hand, crossed my arm and glared at Marcus. "Mind telling me what's gotten her so worked up?"

"No idea," Marcus said with a twinkle in his eye.

I couldn't help but smile. "You guys planning something I need to know about?"

Marcus raised his hands. "Maybe... maybe not... What I want to know is what you two were planning. I know nothing about a case."

"Well, mister," I said. "Since you know nothing about a case. Then you must know nothing about the vandals, the sudden lack of money for uniforms, the sudden lack of money for a school production, and —"

"Oh, that case," interjected Marcus. "Yeah, of course I heard it." He stepped toward me and placed a hand on his chin. "I'm a detective after all."

"You're such a dork," I said, punching him lightly on the shoulder. "By the way, here's the key. You're driving. I'm starving, and you're buying."

"Whatever you say." Marcus laughed as he opened the backseat of the car and tossed his bag in while I made my way around to the passenger seat. It's a thing we do; he drives my car. It's weird, I know, but he doesn't have his own, and he needs the practice.

Just as Marcus keyed the ignition, a dark jeep pulled up behind us, blocking us in. I groaned, "What now." I turned as the horned blare. Nate and Janice waved at us from the seat. We rolled down our windows.

Nate hit the horn again for good measure and grinned. "Forget about going out tonight. There's a protest down at the board of education. Something about the budget. Get in!"

Marcus and I exchanged a quick glance. "We could always get something to eat over there," he said. "I heard there's this great bistro and —"

"Let's go," I groaned.

After rolling up the windows, Marcus turned the car off. After hopping in the backseat of the Jeep, we quickly buckled. This time, Nate waited until he heard the resounding click before he peeled out of the parking lot.

On the way, I wondered if this thing had anything to do with Marcus' dad being out for the day. With a furrowed brow, Marcus stared intently at his phone. I wondered if he was thinking the same thing. I texted my parents, letting them know where I was going.

* * *

"What's this protest about?" Marcus asked, voicing precisely what I'd been thinking.

From the driver's seat, Nate glanced at Marcus. "Board meeting in a few weeks. Something to do with the budget cuts."

"It's more of a rally, then?" Marcus asked.

I nudged Marcus. "Maybe your dad might be there."

He checked his phone. "Not so sure. He didn't respond to my text."

Several car lengths behind us, someone laid on their horn, causing the four of us to jump.

"Seriously," Janice shouted to no one. "Where's that guy think we're all going."

She was right, of course. With the cover off, I was feeling the heat of the sun. Like everyone else, we were in a standstill on the only two-lane county road leading into town.

I spotted an empty space in a parking lot and got an idea I knew Nate would be keen on. "Let's hop the curb and park over there."

Nate spun the wheel. The Jeep bumped once, then twice over the curb. While we were being jostled about, a faded blue sedan crept toward our spot.

"Not so fast, pal," Nate grinned and stomped on the gas, causing the engine to roar and the tires to squeal as he cut in front of the sedan. I made eye-contact with a wide-eyed older man who slammed on his breaks.

Janice laughed as Marcus looked around.

"Good thing there weren't any cops around," Marcus said.

As the driver of van shook his fist at us, I shrank into my seat. "Yeah," I said. "Good thing. Though, that guy isn't about to move anytime soon."

"Doesn't have to," Nate said. He and Janice unfasten their seatbelts. "C'mon, we've got a protest to catch."

With ease, they hopped out of the Jeep, while Marcus and I climbed out with more deliberation.

The older man in the sedan rolled his window down and shouted, "You kids!"

"Sir," I began. "Sorry, I —

Marcus pulled me away by linking his arm into my own.

"Don't worry about him," Marcus said under his breath.

"You two good?" Nate said, turning toward us while walking backward.

I glanced behind me. The old man pulled his car into a parking spot. Giving Nate two thumbs up, I said, "We're good!"

"Good!" Nate grinned, speaking with enthusiasm. "I was thinking. Maybe we could split up in pairs. You know, scout out the place. Rub shoulders with some of the teachers and bigwigs who might be here. See what we can find out. That sort of thing."

I tugged at Marcus' arm, still linked in my own.

"Sounds good," Marcus said. "Alissa and I are going to catch some grub first at Mammie's Café."

"They've got a great Ruben," Nate said. "We can all hang out if—"

I shot Janice a pleading glance. She got the message. "Nathan," she cooed. "They're good. We can just grab a coffee, okay."

Confusion passed quickly over Nate's face. "Fine, just remember—"

"Bro," Marcus said. He had a hint of irritation in his voice. "We've got this."

Though I didn't need him to speak up, I was glad he did. Nate tends to lose all sense of everything else when he gets into investigative work. He needed Marcus there to pull him back to reality.

Nate nodded. "Got it! We'll see you in a bit."

He and Janice turned and walked toward a gathering crowd a block away.

Marcus pulled gently on my arm. "Let's cut across this way."

With the oncoming traffic still going at a breakneck speed of zero, we had no problem getting across.

"You'd think everyone's going to this thing," I said.

Marcus shrugged. "You'd think we would've known about it. I wonder if that's where my dad was today. Maybe he was organizing, but he didn't tell me anything on the way to school."

"Seems like he would've told you about this protest," I said. "I wonder how Nate found out."

"You know Nate," Marcus grinned. "He probably overheard some teachers talking. I've seen him walk right into the teacher's lounge and strike up a conversation."

"Sounds about right," I offered, though without enthusiasm. As we walked into Mammie's Café, I realized I didn't know much about Nate at all. Sure, the four of us hung out a lot, and he was a good guy, but something about him always seemed just a little mysterious. As we sat at the table, I glanced out the front door, at the traffic beginning to move on the road. Maybe mysterious wasn't the word to describe Nate, but he was definitely tinged with a bit of shadiness. Always up to something on the very edge of the periphery.

* * *

After eating, we headed toward the rally. Ahead of us, a surprisingly large crowd had formed. Those who gathered waved red and white printed or hand-stenciled signs that read, "Teachers made your job possible," "I find your lack of funds disturbing," or "Flunk us! Flunk you!"

I laughed. "That's a clever one." I pointed to the older woman, holding the *Flunk you* sign. "I wonder if she'll know anything."

"Maybe," Marcus said, still grinning from the humor in the sign. "Maybe we can find out who the union leader is, too."

"Hey, kids!" A man said. He wore a red ball cap stitched with white lettering: *Stand With Teachers*. An apple pin hung precariously on the brim. The man stuffed a pamphlet into our hands. "Glad you can make it out. It's so good to see the student body is taking an interest."

Usually, I would've labeled a guy like this way too pushy, but something in the pamphlet caught my attention. "Says here we've had budget cuts for the last seven years," I said.

"That's right," the man said. "You kids might've noticed an increase in class sizes and a decrease in course offerings, too."

"A little," Marcus said. "To be honest, I only notice when the teachers complain."

I added, "And when I can't get into a class I need for graduation. Right now, we're juniors, but some girls on my team complained about having to take a course online to fill the credit requirement."

The man nodded with so much enthusiasm, I thought the apple pin would pop right off the brim of his hat. "Let me tell you," he said. "It's going to get worse. I teach at Patterson High School. It's bad. Look here on page three."

He snatched the pamphlet from me even though he had plenty of his own in his hands. He flipped through a few pages, then handed it back to me. Marcus and I took a look at an impressive graph showing the increase in county residents over the years, but a decrease in educational funding.

"You said you're at Patterson?" I asked, recalling the team, the Buccaneers, we were supposed to play next week.

The man nodded. "Science for almost twenty years. If I could leave, I would. But I'll lose more than I'll gain by switching to a different school district."

Not interested, I thought to myself. "Right," I said. "I'm wondering about how this all affects after school activities."

"Like chess club?" The man asked.

"No, like sports," Marcus said. "Uniforms and out of district games."

I added, thinking of Janice. "And drama productions. Those sorts of things."

The man took off his hat and scratched his head. "I see." He paused for a moment. "I'm not sure, but I know our teams got new uniforms this year. I haven't heard anything about any trips being canceled."

"That's interesting," Marcus said. "Because—"

I yanked Marcus away, cutting him off. "Thanks," I said to the man and waved the pamphlet. "This material is super helpful."

I turned to Marcus and whispered. "Do you know what this means?"

He nodded. "Our problem seems to only be in our school. But how?"

"I don't know," I said. But an idea was beginning to form.

"There they are," Janice called. I turned in her direction. She and Nate were pushing their way through a sea of red-shirted adults. Oddly, they were carrying slogan signs.

"What are those?" Marcus asked. "Souvenirs or something?"

Nate shook his head. "Some teachers from our school gave them to us."

Janice set her sign down next to a trash can. "We also saw Principal Moss, but he was beelining it into the building."

"Was he participating in the rally?" I asked.

"And did you happen to see my dad?" Marcus asked. "I still haven't been able to get a hold of him. On text, or on the phone."

Nate and Janice both shook their heads. "Sorry, guys," Nate said. "This was a bust."

"Not entirely," Marcus said. "Seems our little problem is specific to our school."

I chewed my lower lip and narrowed my eyes. Janice looked at me. "Lis," she said. "I know that look. What're you thinking?"

"Nor sure yet. But something to do with our accounting project. Maybe interviewing someone who would know about how budgets work."

Marcus, Nate, and Janice all looked at each other, totally not comprehending the shred of an idea I introduced to them. Then, like a ray of sunshine peeking out from behind a grey cloud, Nate began to slowly nod his head. The others did the same.

I sort of had a plan. Now, we just needed the right amount of research so we could formulate the right questions to ask the right person.

Chapter Nine

Marcus

After the rally, Nate dropped Alissa and me off at the school. As I rode in the passenger seat of Alissa's Nissan, I couldn't help but notice her intense silence. She stared straight ahead, tightly gripping the steering wheel and biting her lower lip. I knew better than to interrupt her thoughts. When we finally pulled into her driveway, with furrowed brows, she turned to me.

"Marcus," she said. "Please tell me what's going on. At the beach, your dad drank a lot. Then today, he wasn't in school. No way he's okay."

My hand trembled as I thought about Mom in tears last week. I sighed, trying to steady myself. "He probably took off so my parents could take care of this money problem."

"But you don't believe that, do you?" Alissa asked.

"I don't know what to think," I said. "Maybe. They've never told me about money problems before."

"Neither have my parents," Alissa said.

"Is that something they'd share?" I asked.

Alissa thought for a moment, then turned to me. "No. I guess not."

I nodded, then changed the subject. "Tell me about this accounting project you're working on?"

"Not much to tell," Alissa said. "We just got it the other day. Something to do with creating a fictitious business with a year's worth of profit and losses. I thought Janice and I could use the school district, especially since their records are public."

"Sounds interesting," I said.

"No, it sounds super boring," Alissa laughed as she unbuckled her seat belt and turned off the car. "Honestly, the whole class is kind of boring."

"You know what, though," I said, pulling out the pamphlet we got from the rally. "Maybe you'll discover why the school district keeps cutting the budget every year."

She snorted. "Not likely. But it's worth a try."

Just then, there was a knock on my window. I turned to see my sister, Bri.

I sighed. Allissa and I both got out of the car.

"What's up, sissy," Alissa asked. She's been calling Bri *sissy* for years. In many ways, they are like sisters, which is still kind of weird for me.

Bri crinkled her nose. "I hope you two weren't planning on making out."

I felt my face grow hot. "Not really any of your business." But I knew the conversation hadn't been headed in that direction anyway.

"Mom and Dad said you need to get inside right now," Bri said. "Family meeting."

"Alright," I said. "I'll be in a minute."

As Bri traipsed off, Alissa and I grabbed our bags from the backseat of her car. After closing the door, Alissa stood in front of me, her bag slung over her shoulder. With wide, dark eyes, she looked at me.

"Promise you'll tell me what's going on."

"Yeah," my voice cracked. "I will."

We gave each other a silent nod and parted ways.

Definitely not making the top ten list of ways to say goodnight to your belle or beau.

* * *

The living room was less than inviting as Bri and I were greeted by my parents' grim faces. Standing, Dad motioned for us to sit on the sofa. When I sat, Bri took the seat directly next to me even though she had plenty of room to her left. Dad sat at the wing chair opposite my mom.

I didn't wait for Dad to speak. "Where were you today?" I asked.

Dad raised his eyebrows. "It's complicated. I'm on administrative leave."

"But you've led the athletic department forever," I heard myself whine. "You've built it from nothing. All of the teams are in the playoffs every year. We're even nationally ranked. How could they put you on leave?"

Dad held up a hand. "Money. Something's wrong with the bookkeeping. Some money is missing."

Marcus

The word 'missing' hit me like a foul ball across the face. Dad is the most honest guy I know. Once, at a sporting goods store, he told the cashier to re-ring his order when it came up at what I thought to be a discounted price. Sure enough, a jacket that had already been bagged had missed the scanner. Dad could've gotten a fifty-dollar jacket for free. When I left the store with him, I was in awe.

But now I was in shock. I thought about how Patterson High's programs weren't being affected by the district-wide cuts. About the break-in at the ticket booth, then the open boxes in Dad's office, and the money problems my parents are apparently having. A lump that had been forming in my throat seemed to sink all the way down to my gut.

Principal Moss was at the rally today, headed right into the main offices. Dad's ramblings on the ride into school and Dunbar taking Dad's classes today all made sense now.

I swallowed. "Do they think you stole the money?"

Dad shook his head. "I don't know what to think," he said, letting himself sink back in his chair. His voice seemed to do the same as he spoke. "I turned everything in. I was with the office manager as she signed the paperwork."

I'd never seen him this way.

In almost a whisper because I didn't want to ask the question any more than I wished to hear the answer. "Does Moss think you stole it?"

Mom said, "No sweetie, of course not..."

Dad rambled on, keeping me from asking the real question. "Maybe the finance office is wrong," he said. "Maybe something was lost between my hands and the deposit. Maybe..."

Mom stood up. "It's something you and Bri don't need to worry about. We've got savings, and I'm still on the PTSA. The union's behind your father. They've got lawyers. It's probably just a simple mistake. They'll catch it, and he'll be back to work in no time. You'll see." Mom flashed us a tight smile when she finished.

"What if it doesn't work out?" I asked.

"Let's hope it doesn't come to that," Mom said.

But, hey," Dad said. "If things don't work out, I've got something lined up at the pizza shop down the road." Dad laughed dryly. I couldn't tell whether he was joking.

Mom glanced at him, then directed her attention entirely on us as if Dad wasn't even in the room. "Why don't you two get ready for school tomorrow?" She asked.

I wanted to protest, to stay there and help them figure things out.

"Do as your mother says," Dad said. "Homework doesn't stop just because I'm not going into school for a while."

"Yes, sir." Bri and I responded in unison.

Bri and I began to head up the steps.

"Marcus," Mom called. "How was the rally? "

I blinked several times, trying to process everything going on. Taking a deep breath, I answered, "Very eye-opening."

Mom nodded, and I hid in my bedroom. Alissa and I needed to talk because this new information would have to change the whole direction of her research.

* * *

"That does change everything," Alissa said.

We sat on the back steps of her house, where I filled her in on everything I learned. It had been well-past eleven p.m. when I texted Alissa. I snuck out when I was sure my parents had finally gone to bed.

She scooted closer to me until I felt the warmth of her side against my own. She put an arm around me, and I returned the gesture. I needed this moment to last forever, but I knew it couldn't.

"Have you found anything out about the budget, yet?" I asked.

"Not yet," Alissa said. "I did a search on the district website and found a few things, but I'll need another set of eyes on it. I'm not entirely sure what I'm looking at."

"All of us can pitch in," I said.

"I know," Alissa said. "But, given what you just told me about your dad, I think you should take the lead on this investigation."

I nodded, knowing full well what she meant. Nate had a lot of good ideas, but sometimes they were incredibly impulsive and out-right dangerous. Besides, this was my dad we were talking about, not some random person. Something was definitely off at Lenape High, and I was glad to have Alissa by my side to help me clear Dad's name and get him back to work.

I squeezed her tighter. She smiled. Her eyes seemed to sparkle in the glow of the incandescent bulb. I gazed at her, leaning closer to her until I felt a tickle at the back of my neck. I slapped a moth away.

"Thanks, Lis," I said. "You know, for being here."

"Where else would I go?" She grinned. "I've got your back."

We stayed there, silently communing with the other, breathing in each other's presence. In the distance, a dog barked, and a door slammed shut. I felt my eyes grow heavy and fought to keep my head from bobbing.

"Alright, sleepy-head," Alissa said. "See ya in the morning."

"Yeah," I said with a yawn as we stood. "See ya."

Though I was definitely tired, that night, I tossed and turned as images of my dad sneaking about the high school formed in my head. I tried to push back the thought that he'd be the one to skim money, but I also knew that anyone, including my dad, could steal if they were desperate enough to do so. I wondered how long we'd been having money problems. I simultaneously wished tonight's moment with Alissa could've lasted forever.

Chapter Ten

Alissa

Marcus and I poured over some old financial reports while Nate and Janice did some research on one of the school library computers. In the hour before practice started, we all agreed, with Marcus' insistence, and Janice's and Nate's grumbling, we'd meet after school. To describe our research as grueling would've been an understatement.

"Hey guys," Janice called from a study carol in the school library. "Look what we found."

Marcus and I set our things down and joined Janice and Nate. Janice scrolled through a numbered list.

"Slow down," Marcus said. "I don't know what you're showing us."

"Here," Nate said, increasing the size of the screen. "Is that better?"

Marcus and I hovered over their shoulders as we leaned in.

"It's the school's proposed budget this school year," I said. "Where'd you find this?"

Rolling her eyes, Janice said, "Seriously. Does no one do research anymore? You can find it on the school district's website."

*She had a poin*t, I thought. I had glanced at the site a few days ago but didn't get back to it until today. Honestly, I didn't want to just Google my research, like a lot of people do today. Even worse, a lot of people today react without doing any more research beyond Google.

I sighed. "Getting the district's budget can't be that easy," I said. "Can we take a look?"

Nate and Janice stood while Marcus and I took their seats. I stared at the screen for a moment before I began to click through some hyperlinks.

Marcus said, "This looks a lot more complicated than the simple spreadsheet we saw at camp this summer."

I shuddered. "And now the camp's closed down. This here's legit."

Or, maybe it wasn't, I thought as I clicked back to the list of twenty-four items while the others looked over my shoulder. I spotted the Extra-Curricular Activities Section and clicked.

"Stop there," Marcus said, pointing to athletics. "Maybe that'll show us something."

I clicked the hyperlink and said with sarcasm, "Maybe someone left a sign pointing to overspending on miscellaneous supplies."

Marcus frowned. "You're right. It can't be that obvious."

"Or that easy," Janice said.

Sensing the complete deflation of hope in all of them, I turned. The three of them stared at me with eyes hungry for more information. My friends seemed capable of holding their breaths for as long as it took to get the information they sought. I looked back at the website and clicked on a document titled Business Services Section. Again, just a lot of numbers.

"Honestly," I said, keeping my eyes focused on the screens in front of me. "I really don't know what I'm looking at. I mean, here and there spending increases or decreases, but that's millions of dollars."

Marcus looked away. Janice and Nate blinked a few times. Janice spoke, "So, no case?"

I chewed my bottom lip for a moment. "I wouldn't say that. That's a quick glance. We'd have to print out every document and examine each one more closely."

"I'm down with that," Marcus said. "How about you guys?"

"Bro," Nate said. "We are so down with that. This case is going to be epic."

Marcus and Nate fist-bumped.

I laughed. "I hoped you guys would be up for this. We need all the help we can get."

"Lis," Janice said. "I'll staple the copies over here. Print everything, okay?"

As the printer whirred to life, Marcus stood.

"I've got an idea," he said with enthusiasm. "What if we printed these reports and brought them to Principal Moss. We tell him we're doing an accounting project or something."

Nate's eyes lit up. "We could go over the report and ask a few questions like we're doing some research for the project. Maybe he could give us more information without knowing."

"Excuse me," I said. "Who's this 'we' you're referring to?"

Nate pointed to himself and Marcus.

Marcus stepped away from him. "Moss is a smart guy, you know. I'm pretty sure he'll figure out why I'm there."

"That's what I was thinking," I said. "Besides, neither of you are taking an accounting class. Janice and I will go."

Nate grumbled about the girls taking charge, but I ignored him and hit print on the next document. Suddenly, the librarian, who had been shelving books, came over to Nate.

"How many copies are you kids making?" She asked.

The resounding smack of a stapler caught my attention. I looked back at the librarian, "This one's only ten pages."

Marcus added, "We'll be finished up soon. We, um, shouldn't have to print any more than thirty pages."

"It's for a class project," I said. "I don't have a printer at home."

The librarian narrowed her eyes. "I don't usually let students do any more than ten, but I'll make an exception..."

"Thank you." My voice cracked. I wasn't sure what to say next. The librarian stared intently at us, so I remained quiet.

"Make sure you're finished printing in half an hour, okay?" she asked. She walked away.

"Marcus," I said. "Go on another computer and print the other documents. Janice, you and Nate got that?"

"Yup," she said, slamming the stapler down on another pack. "We're on it."

"Looks like we've got a busy couple of days," Marcus said. "Let's hope Moss'll see you."

I took a deep breath. I'd never actually spoken directly to our school principal. About him, yes. All of us did, but very few of us actually sat across from him in his office. "Good thing Janice'll be along with me."

"It'll suck to do it alone," Marcus said, voicing my sentiment.

"We've got a lot riding on this, so the next couple days," I raised my voice so Janice and Nate could hear. "The four of us make —"

"The squad!" Nate and Janice chanted as they cut me off. "We know."

I rolled my eyes. My friends knew me too well. That's... a good thing.

When Marcus and I printed the last of our reports, which came to way more than thirty pages, we all stood.

"Alright, guys," Marcus said. "Sometime this week, Alissa will make an appointment with

Moss. Then, we'll meet Saturday morning and get something together."

As we headed to practice, Janice handed me the paperwork. "Here," she said. "You better hold on to these. I might lose them in the theatre."

"So, the play's back on?" I asked her.

"Nope," she said. "But I'll be able to work *When You're Home* into our variety show."

"That's awesome," I said. "I know I've heard it a million times, but I can't wait to hear it on stage."

She grinned. Things were looking up for Janice and the drama program. That gave me a lot of hope for the sports program, especially when it came to our soccer uniforms.

* * *

I pounded the soccer ball, sending it sailing across the field and into the opposing goal. An impressive play, especially for a sweeper.

"Yeah, Lis! Use that on the Buccaneers next week," one of my teammates called as we retook our starting positions.

I grinned. "I plan too!"

We were playing a Varsity / Junior Varsity mixed team scrimmage and, not to brag, but my team was in the lead.

Alissa

From the sidelines, the shrill vibration of Coach Becky's whistle blew, calling us all to bring our scrimmage to a halt. Several of us groaned. Still, we jogged to the sidelines and plopped ourselves in the grass or on the bench as we gulped water, waiting for Coach Becky's instruction. By her side stood the JV Coach, a teacher at our school named Mrs. Moreau.

As I took a long gulp, Dunbar trotted down the sidelines, his belly jiggling until he seemed to force himself into our little group.

"Nice playing, ladies," Dunbar said, still catching his breath. "Bring that, plus some, when you play the Buccaneers." He placed his hands on his hips. With a smile, he seemed to make eye-contact with each of us in a silent congratulatory nod.

We, in turn, returned his gesture with blank stares. I imagined my teammates, JV girls included, had the same thought going through their minds: *What's this wanna-be doing rolling up on us like this at practice?*

Coach Becky turned her gaze from Dunbar to Mrs. Moreau. Our coaches shared a pained expression. Mrs. Moreau sighed. "I'm sure you've all heard Mr. Kahale is on a leave of absence. As you know, Mr. Dunbar is covering his classes. That also includes overseeing the whole of the athletic department."

She said this last part with about as much gusto as us girls, who dreaded our P.E. classes with Mr. Dunbar. Dunbar filling in for Mr. Kahale's classes made sense. Though, I could list several, including Coach Becky or Mrs. Moreau, who would be better qualified to oversee the whole department in Kahale's absence.

Several hands shot up. Then the questions followed.

When's Kahale coming back?

How long are you going to be the acting director?

When're we going to get new uniforms?

Mr. Dunbar held his hands out with palms down in a gesture to get us a quiet. "Whoah!" He grinned and turned to our coaches. "You told me they're a lively group, but... Anyway, girls," he turned back to us. "I'm not at liberty to tell you about Mr. Kahale, but I can answer one of your questions. Unfortunately, you won't be getting your uniforms this year."

With a cacophony of complaints, the girls protested. I spoke up, quieting them down, "JV's already wearing ancient uniforms. Uniforms cost, what? Sixty bucks each. What happened to our order?"

I swear Dunbar shot me an icy glare. In a flash, his expression softened.

Coach Becky stepped closer to us. With a low voice, she spoke, "Sometimes things come up. This just isn't our year for new uniforms."

"What if the PTSA pitched in?" I asked, thinking about Mrs. Kahale's direct and indirect involvement in just about every after-school program at school.

Coach Becky and Mrs. Moreau seemed to look to Dunbar for some kind of approval, which didn't seem at all appropriate since he was only a substitute.

Dunbar nodded. "Tell ya what. I'll run it up the chain of command and see what we can do. For now, though," he paused, then shouted. "Let's hear it for the Warriors!"

He put his hand out, palm down, expecting us to do the same. One girl awkwardly extended her hand but withdrew it quickly when no one else joined her. Coach Becky cleared her throat and looked right at me. Reluctantly, I uncrossed my arms and reached my right hand out. Mentally cringing, I placed my hand over Dunbar's hand. The other girls did the same.

"On three," I shouted, forcing as much authentic enthusiasm as I could into my cheer. I began, shouting, "One, two, three." In unison, we cheered. "Warriors!"

Admittedly, it felt good to cheer with my teammates, both on JV and Varsity. Once again, we ran out to the field. My team had the ball. When the whistle blew, the forwards ran the ball down the field to the opposing goal. I stole a glance at Coach Becky and Mrs. Moreau. They watched the play with intensity, taking vigorous notes. Then, out of the corner of my eye, I saw Dunbar looking my way. With crossed arms and a smirk on his face, he nodded at me. Though I refused to look directly at him, he directed an almost imperceptible thumbs-up in my direction.

The gesture, an apparent silent approval of my reluctant support of his leadership, threw me off. So much so, I nearly slipped as I swung a leg at an oncoming ball. I missed, but my goalie caught the ball, made a short sprint, and kicked it off.

"You okay, Lis?" she asked.

"Yeah, I'm good," I said.

"If you say so," she replied, clearly unconvinced. "Just don't do that tomorrow."

"No need to worry about that," I said with a laugh. "Dunbar won't be there to distract us."

My goalie laughed. "Let's hope not!"

Honestly, I shared the same sentiment. But, even if Dunbar did come to the game, it would be my fault if I let him distract me again.

Chapter Eleven

Marcus

Very few things made me feel freer than when I ran cross country. I made no distinction between a practice or a meet. I needed the wind in my hair and my feet pounding the ground more than ever. With my team gathered around me, I stretched, elongating muscles and alleviating the stress of school while trying to figure out some way to clear Dad's name.

In mid-stretch, I knelt down, taking my frustration out on my shoelaces with a quick tug. At home, Dad and Mom were more than just a little off. I wasn't convinced they were "fine" as they claimed. Standing, I glanced up at Bri. She sat in the bleachers. Per usual, she had her face buried in her phone. Her being here, instead of at home, served to prove the point I made to myself. Things weren't okay at home. Just before practice, Mom sent me a text, telling me Bri would meet me here, then ride home with Alissa and me.

The whistle blew, calling us to take our places at the starting line.

They're just meeting with lawyers, I told myself. The whistle blew again. My muscles took over, driving me further away from the starting point, from worry, and from Bri's texting. Only to focus on putting distance between myself and the runners behind me while simultaneously pacing myself for the 5k in front of me.

Our track led around the football field, now empty for an away game. Dad would've been there, but...

"To your left!" A runner behind me huffed.

I smirked, letting the JV runner pass me. I knew he'd regret it in about three minutes when

I smoked past him. In another moment, I caught a glimpse of the soccer fields where Alissa played with her team, only they weren't playing. Instead, they were huddled in a circle with their coaches and... Dunbar?

"On your right!" Another runner said as he passed me.

I let the varsity runner have it. That is, until out of the corner of my eye, I spotted the old shed, its door wide open. The lock, I figured should've been fixed by now. Then, I spotted Mrs. Johnson, our assistant principal, exiting the ticket booth. I wondered what she could possibly be doing. Maybe she was assessing the damage and reporting back to Moss. She seemed to be carrying something in her hand. From where I jogged, it wasn't possible to get a good look. But I could've sworn there was nothing in the shed when Nate and I checked it out earlier. Then again, I didn't have the time to be thorough, either. I thought back to Dad's urgency in questioning me about what I saw in the ticket booth. Then Moss practically pouncing on Nate and me on Monday so we could fill out some incident reports.

Suddenly, I realized I had stopped running altogether. So much for absolute freedom.

"Kahale! Get a move on!" Coach's shout came to me from a distance. Realizing all but one player had passed me, I turned and hauled ass, catching up to all but the lead runner before we finished for time.

"Eighteen and fifty-eight seconds," Coach shouted as I passed him.

After catching my breath and stretching, I grabbed a bottle and gulped down some water. I couldn't believe my stalling cost me over two minutes off my standard practice time. But at least I didn't come in last place.

Coach marched up to me when the last runner finished. His red face told me he had different opinions about my placement. "Kahale!" He shouted. "You want to be bumped down to JV? What happened out there?"

"Sorry, coach," I mumbled. "I was... distracted."

"I saw," he said. "Looked like you were a damn scarecrow."

"It won't happen again."

Instead of responding, he turned to the rest of the team. "Alright, boys. Bring it in. Big match coming up."

Some of the others eyed me for a moment before turning their full attention back to Coach. I didn't care. While leading in cross country was a big deal for me, seeing Johnson heading away from the ticket booth took first place. Nate and

Marcus

I had missed something that seemed to be a pretty big deal. I didn't know what.

As soon as Coach dismissed us, Bri hopped off the bleachers. Before she could reach me, I grabbed my phone and shot a text to Nate: *What time does Johnson usually leave?*

"Wow!" Bri's obnoxious sarcasm greeted me as she walked up. "You really stunk it up out there."

I ignored her and read the text from Nate: *Still here after drama lets out at six. Why?*

I smiled at Bri. "Something's come up. Meet Alissa down at the parking lot and ride home with her."

Bri crossed her arms. "Really? And what am I supposed to tell Mom and Dad?"

"Tell them I'm studying," I said. I groaned as Bri scowled at me. "I'll give you five dollars next time we go out," I pleaded.

"Make it ten," she said.

"Fine, ten."

"Sucker," Bri laughed. Turning on her heels, she took off toward the parking lot where I knew Alissa would be waiting for us.

I shot Alissa a text: *Riding with Nate. There's been a development. Will fill you in.*

Then to Nate: *Ready for a stakeout?*

Shadows of Doubt

* * *

Nate and I sat in a booth at Nick's Pizza and Subs right across the street from the school. We'd been sitting there for almost an hour, watching the school parking lot. From where we positioned ourselves, we could see the entire faculty parking lot, plus the front entrance and southside maintenance entrance to the building. Mrs. Johnson's car, a white BMW, hadn't moved. Neither had Moss' SUV, a dark blue Mercedes.

Across from me, Nate took a long slurp of soda, shook the ice, then took another slurp.

"You want a refill?" I asked as I stood.

He grinned. "You bet. Gotta stay awake for these *study* sessions."

Taking his cup, and mine, I went to the soda fountain. Honestly, I had no idea what I expected to find on this impromptu stakeout. I knew I was operating on a thin shred of circumstantial evidence. For all I knew, Mrs. Johnson could've been rekeying the ticket booth, though I didn't see anyone else with her. With our cups refilled, I returned to our table. As I sat and shifted in my seat, the worn pleather beneath me crackled and creaked. This seat needed some serious attention, sort of like this case.

As Nate stared out the window, I checked my messages. One from my parents asked what time I'd be home. Another from Alissa asked if I wanted her to join me. *Heck ya*, I wanted to write back, but Nate and I agreed it would be just the two of us tonight. Partly, I didn't admit out-loud, was because we wanted to save ourselves from the potential embarrassment of finding nothing. Alissa and Janice would've ragged on us for a while before they decided to let it go.

"Maybe we should call it quits for the night?" I offered.

Nate, eyes still focused on the school building, craned his neck forward and squinted. "Did you bring binoculars?"

"Why?" I asked, directing my attention out the window as well.

Moss' SUV was on the move, leaving Johnson's BMW alone in the parking lot. The SUV crept past the front entrance, then backed up to the maintenance entrance. Moss, I assumed to be the driver, flashed his lights once.

"What do you think is going on?" I asked.

Nate put a finger up and shushed me as the maintenance entrance opened. From this distance, I couldn't make out the two figures exiting the building, but I could tell they carried boxes in their hands.

Nate, with wide, wild eyes, turned toward me. "Tell me you wanna get a closer look."

I stood, giving him my answer. Leaving our unfinished soda and tip, we exited Nick's and ran down the block, south of the front entrance. There we crossed the street. Keeping the maintenance entrance in our peripheral, we zipped through a patch of grass. Once we hit the school, we glued ourselves to the outside wall, where we listened and waited.

Beside me, Nate breathed heavily. Above his breathing, the door of a vehicle clicked open. Then I heard two distinct voices.

"There's still a lot left," Moss said.

"That's all we can fit tonight," Johnson answered. "Let's do this again on Wednesday. Maybe put some of it into my car."

"Good idea," Moss said. "We need a drink after this."

"You buying?" Johnson asked playfully.

Their conversation came to a pause. A door rattled and clicked.

"Hey, uh, 'scuse me," came a male voice, deep and garbled, like there was food in his mouth.

"What is it now?" Johnson asked, not even trying to hide her irritation.

"Just, uh, seein' if you still need the door open," the male voice came again. He forced a laugh. "You know. Gotta lock up for the night."

"You can lock it," Moss said. "We'll get the rest later."

In the school's shadows, Nate and I remained, listening and waiting for more. A car door slammed; the Mercedes started up. We watched it pull out of the parking lot. For another few minutes, Nate and I stared at each other in the darkness, not daring to move. Holding our proverbial breaths, we waited for Johnson to leave.

In my head, I counted *one-one-thousand, two-one-thousand, three-one-thousand...* until I got to *three-hundred-one-thousand*. Surely, she'd be gone after five minutes.

I was about to peek around the corner when a phone rang.

"Yeah," Johnson said when she answered. "I'm heading out... I thought I heard someone, but I don't know. See ya. Bye."

The sound of her heels clicking against the pavement faded further from us. In the distance, her car started-up. Soon after, we got visual confirmation that we were indeed alone. Johnson headed South in her BMW.

"Whoa," Nate said. "That's heavy."

Turning to him, I blinked my eyes several times, adjusting to a small, bright light. With a penlight in his mouth to illuminate a small notebook he had in his lap, Nate wrote vigorously.

As I waited out his moment of notetaking, I shot Alissa a text: *Heavy stuff to share.*

Alissa: *Can't wait to hear. BTW. Got an email from Moss' secretary. Gonna meet with him tomorrow. 7 a.m. Anything I need to know?*

"Got it," Nate cheered as he stood, flicking off his flashlight.

"But what does it all mean?" I asked, knowing what we just witnessed couldn't be accounted as anything other than circumstantial. "For all we know, they could be doing some house cleaning."

"Sure," Nate said. "And we could be the groundskeepers hanging out at —" he pulled my phone toward him — "8:37 at night."

I swallowed hard. "We've gotta go. The other guy said he'd be locking up soon."

"No prob," Nate said. "We'll need to plan fast, though. Moss and Johnson said they're doing this again on Wednesday.

"Doesn't give us much time to plan," I said as we hiked up the slope. "Better than tomorrow night," Nate said. "We've got this!"

Marcus

Bumping fists, we darted across the street. As Nate drove me home, we speculated on various scenarios. By the time we got to my house, we had a solid plan we could pitch to the girls. I just hoped they'd be game for it.

Chapter Twelve

Alissa

"Mr. Moss," Mrs. Heinemann, the principal's secretary, called through her receiver. "Two young ladies, Alissa Claude and Janice Kane are here to see you."

Alissa

Seven in the morning Janice and I stood in the front office. I tightly clutched the folder of accounting files in my hand as I waited for Mrs. Heinemann's reply.

"Okay, go ahead, you two," she said with a smile. "His office is two doors down the hall and on your left."

Beside me, Janice, eyes darting from one photograph on the wall to another, avoided making a single comment.

"Girl," I said. "Lighten up. Two of us can't be nervous."

Janice let out a breath. "Want to hear a joke?'

"Yes," I said. "But after the meeting, okay?"

Moss stood up as we stepped into his office. His brilliant smile seemed to spread across the whole of his face.

"Alissa, Janice," he said, shaking each of our hands when he said our names. "Take a seat. What can I do for you two?"

Fumbling with my paperwork, I cleared my throat. "We're doing this accounting project. I'm using the school district as a model. But I'm stuck on a few things. I'm hoping you could help."

I handed him my folder while Janice and I sat across his desk. Moss took it and began looking over one of the many sheets of paper we'd printed. His eyes, magnified by his boxy metal-framed glasses, seemed to glide across the paper. I was totally expecting him to hand the documents back to us and tell us we needed to get ready for class.

Moss removed his glasses and rubbed his eyes. "What do you want to know about the budget for Curriculum and Instruction?"

"Supplies," I said. "How does the school show the district they purchased what they said they purchased?'

He smiled. "You must be referring to that case where the secretary was caught with theft of over one-hundred-fifty thousand."

Janice shot me a glance, mouth gaping. I nodded and lied, "I am. How does that happen?"

"Remind me again what this accounting project is all about." Principal Moss' gaze remained unwavering.

Janice spoke enthusiastically. "We're creating a fictitious profit and loss report for the year that would pass an audit," she said. "We thought it'll be best if we began studying the school budget. It's the easiest to access and the most relevant."

Principal Moss glanced back at me, harrumphed, then directed his attention back to Janice.

He set the papers down and removed his glasses. "Tell me what you want to know."

Janice cleared her throat. "Everything in the budget has to be accounted for, right?"

Principal Moss looked at her. He was waiting for more.

"Right," I said. "Who holds each school accountable?"

"There's an annual audit," Principal Moss began. "It's a real nightmare. A team from central office comes in and reviews all of our receipts and invoices. If something is off even slightly, they question it."

I took a breath, processing that information. "What if it's off by a penny?"

"Even then," Principal Moss said. "We have to give an account. But *off* usually means there's a missing receipt, or a form not properly filled out."

Supplies, I realized, really couldn't be fudged. I flipped over my copy of the budget. "What about these 'other charges'? It marks things like mileage, professional dues, and conferences. Is the school district really planning on reimbursing over thirty-three thousand dollars to employees for travel?"

"I shouldn't be telling you this," Principal Moss said as he leaned in. "But it's for your project. Last year alone, I was reimbursed for almost one thousand dollars for travel and professional development."

I took a couple of notes to buy myself some time. I didn't expect Principal Moss to be so straight with us.

"Wow!" Janice said. "Is that normal?"

Principal Moss lowered his voice to a little more than a whisper. "If anything, the school district doesn't have budget enough. A lot of us still pay out of pocket for various expenses, even when it's school-related."

"The district runs a tight ship," I said. "Still, people get away with theft. How's that a thing?"

"First," Principal Moss said. "I wouldn't call it a 'thing.'" He stood up, went to a filing cabinet, and pulled out a sheet of paper. "Let me give you this."

The paper seemed to float over the desk until it landed in front of us. I nearly gasped when I leaned in to look at it. Janice and I were staring at our high school football team's budget from the last school year. I blinked several times when I saw how much the football program spent on new uniforms. I couldn't believe they spent thirteen thousand dollars. Though I felt girls' soccer was getting shafted, I had to let it go and try to process the rest of the report.

"I think you girls are thinking too big about this accounting project," Principal Moss said. "Seeing it on a smaller scale might help."

Before I could get a good look at the rest of the numbers, several more similar documents floated across the desk.

Principal Moss sat down and raised his eyebrows. "Well?" He asked like he was expecting a reward.

"Thanks," I said.

While Janice asked Principal Moss a few more questions about the budget, I went back to the papers. Two other sections on the football budget caught my attention. I had to be sure I wasn't totally tripping out. Its revenue was $49,161. Its expenses were the same. I wondered if there'd be a similar balance between revenue and expenses on other reports in the same way.

"Excuse me, Principal Moss," I said. He and Janice both looked at me, though their expressions were totally different. She looked relieved, and he looked annoyed.

"These are for us, right?" I asked.

"Of course," Principal Moss said, adding with a wink. "It's for your project, isn't it?"

I nodded. "I noticed the revenue and expenses are the same."

"That's right," Principal Moss said. "Accounts cannot carry over from one year to the next."

"What if they do?" I asked.

Principal Moss stood as he said, "They don't."

Janice stood. "What if they have extra money? Like, they have everything they need, but there's still money left over. Where does that go?"

Principal Moss sighed. "Advisors and coaches are encouraged to use all of their funds. Otherwise, it's reallocated for discretionary spending."

Janice looked at me with a raised eyebrow. I didn't know what discretionary spending meant, either. But Principal Moss seemed ready to bounce. So was I.

"Thank you so much for your help," I said as I stood. "Do you mind if we check in with you at another time?"

"Not a problem," Principal Moss said. "Feel free to make an appointment with Mrs. Heinemann anytime."

Janice and I took our cue from Principal Moss. Our time was up, but that wouldn't mean we'd stop digging.

On our way out, we passed Mrs. Heinemann.

She smiled at us sweetly. "Did you two get what you needed?"

"We did," I said. "Principal Moss said we should follow up with you for further appointments."

Well, okay." Mrs. Heinemann tapped her appointment book. "You know where to find me when you're ready to schedule. Have a lovely day, girls."

Janice and I thanked her and headed out the door. A few students, carrying band equipment, began entering the building. The band teacher hung out at the front door and waved at us.

Janice waved enthusiastically back at her, then turned to me. "So, we've got a ton of time. My nerves are shot. I need coffee."

I laughed. "That sounds good about now. And let's agree not to talk about numbers, okay?"

We did an about-face, passing the band teacher who said with laughter in her voice, "You're headed the wrong way, aren't you?"

"Don't worry," Janice said. "We'll be back in no time."

Once out the door, Janice added. "Speaking of the *wrong-way*. Did you get the feeling that was way too easy?"

"Maybe," I said. "Moss could've been pressed for time. He did know we were coming."

"Or maybe he was covering something up," Janice added.

I shook my head and sighed. "Now, we sound like some conspiracy nuts." Then I paused in thought. We were missing something. "Those discretionary funds seem.... I don't know."

"Unchecked?" Janice asked as we got into my Nissan.

Unchecked, I mentally noted as we pulled out of the parking lot. But we couldn't definitively draw that conclusion with the very little we had to go on. We needed more information. Our best source was Marcus' father, but I was pretty sure he wouldn't be cool with us digging around his business. Just like I was pretty sure he couldn't come through for us on getting our new uniforms, which I desperately needed this afternoon.

* * *

I slammed one ball, then another, as they came at me. Nothing could stop this girl from keeping the Buccaneers from having a chance on goal. I even broke a few ankles as I drove the ball upfield into our offensive lines until I could pass it off to one of our forwards.

"Where'd you get those uniforms?" Number 22, a Buccaneer girl with a thick, black ponytail taunted me. "Hand-me-downs from your grandmother?'

A lot of other lame taunts came at me. But none of them fazed me. If anything, I played harder. The whole team did.

That is, until the same girl came at me again and kicked the ball right at my face, not even aiming for the goal. I got out of the way, hoping our goalie would make the save.

Cheers erupted from the sidelines. Twenty-two sneered. "See ya on the cheap side!"

"Hey, smart one," I yelled back at her. "Cheapside's the financial center of the UK!"

"Whatever," she said. "Your uniforms are still moldy."

That's when I called for a quick time-out. Once the Warrior girls came to a huddle, I gave my pep-talk. "Alright, girls. They're talking crap, but that's because they've got no game. Remember, these uniforms" — I tugged at my jersey — "they don't make the team. We do. Bring it in."

With one hand on the other, we cheered, "One. Two. Three. Warriors!"

Though I really wished those discretionary funds could be used to buy us new uniforms, it didn't matter at the moment. In the end, those Buccaneer girls couldn't measure up to our skills. We crushed it.

At the end of the game, Marcus came up to me.

"Tight playing out there," Marcus said. "Those other girls, though..."

I eyeballed him as I crossed my arms. "What about those other girls?"

Marcus grinned. "Some real trash-talk. Sorry about the uniforms."

"It's okay," I said. "New uniforms are for losers. Maybe next year."

Marcus nodded. "Listen, we've got a thing tomorrow night the four of us have to be at if that's okay."

"No doubt," I said. "Fill me in before then."

Marcus gave me an awkward hug before heading off to the parking lot. He and I seriously needed to work on our own game, and I needed to head off to celebrate with the team. Still, I wondered what Marcus had planned for tomorrow night.

Chapter Thirteen

Marcus

"Seriously, you had me waiting all day for this?" Alissa said, eyeing me. "That's a terrible plan. Not to mention, it's already past seven. We don't want to be out past curfew."

"We're just going to see where they're going," Nate said. "You should be home before eleven. No problem."

We were at Nick's Pizza and Subs across the street from the school.

"I don't see what following them has to do with these budget reports," Alissa waved a wad of papers, emphasizing her points.

Each of us had a handful of papers in front of us. They were much easier to understand than what we got off the district's website.

Nate sat to my left. "These reports don't prove anything," he said, though he didn't sound convincing. "Especially since Moss just handed them to you. We should keep watching Moss. You know, find out what he's up to."

He looked at me, hoping I'd come to his defense. I wanted to help; to do something.

I took a sip of soda, then said, "I'm not really buying into the idea of following Principal Moss, either. Even if we do, what could we possibly gain from that?"

"That's right," Alissa said. "You saw the spending reports he gave us. You're tripping if you think these reports prove he's hiding anything."

Nate was on the defense. "It's not just the reports. It's his behavior," he said. "In about five minutes, he'll be coming out of the building. So will Johnson. You'll see. Here!"

Nate pulled out his notebook, opening it to the page where he transcribed the conversation. He slid it over to Janice and Alissa. They both seemed to be reaching for the notebook as if seeing it for the first time.

Janice's face softened. "This is where you two were the other night. I get it now."

"Get what?" Alissa asked. She shifted in her seat. "Why am I the last to know?"

"That's because..." Nate's voice trailed off when he was arrested by a steely-eyed glance from Alissa.

Janice picked up where Nate apparently left off. "Girl, he didn't want you stealing his thunder."

Alissa sucked in her lower lip. "Oh, honey," she said to Nate. "You were afraid I'd veto your plans."

Nate's jaw dropped as he shifted a glance from Alissa to Janice, then to me. It took a lot of effort on my part to hold in a snicker.

"She's kidding, Nate," I said. "If you want to play *M* to our 007s, that's fine."

"Not *M*," Nate said. "If you haven't noticed, we're supposed to be following your lead."

A lump formed in my throat. "I... okay. But everything we do; we agree as a team."

"No, prob," Alissa grinned.

"Awesome," Nate said. "Take a look over there."

We looked across the street to where he was pointing. As predicted, Moss' Mercedes and Johnson's BMW backed into the side maintenance entrance, which opened. When a man stepped out, Moss and Johnson got out of their own vehicles, entered the building, and returned a few minutes later with boxes they placed in the back of their cars. The three of them, the other man included, returned to the building and exited with more boxes.

"That's our cue," Alissa said. She stood and grabbed my hand and winked. "Marc, this'll be a blast."

On our way out the door, Nate planted his face into his palm and muttered, "Oh, brother." Janice giggled. We were supposed to play it inconspicuous by eavesdropping on Moss and Johnson when they drove up to the shop and entered. Something told me Alissa didn't intend for us to just hang in shadows.

* * *

Once outside, Alissa stepped real close to me. If it weren't for the heat and humidity, I would've liked it. I took a step back.

She bit her lower lip. "While we're out here waiting for Moss and Johnson to come on over, I need to ask you something."

She didn't need to ask; I anticipated what she was going to say. "It's getting worse at home."

Alissa nodded. "That's what I was afraid of. How's Bri taking it?"

I tensed. "I really don't know."

"I'll talk to her," she said. She tilted her head up. "How about you?"

My eyes met hers and lingered there for a moment. They drew me in until my lips, like they were waking up from an afternoon nap, fumbled for hers. I pulled back.

She narrowed her eyes and tightened her lips. She could see right through me.

"We don't have to, you know," she said. "You don't have to pretend like this is going to work. I'm cool with just being friends. I like us either way."

I took a deep breath. "No pretending. I like us, too. Both ways. I was... I had this image of knocking foreheads and slobbering all over your face."

She laughed loudly. "You can't get better at kissing if you don't practice. And I don't mean with a pillow or a CPR dummy. She stepped closer to me and played with a button on my shirt.

Tapping on the windowpane behind us took us out of the moment. Nate glared at us with a sour look on his face while Janice stifled a laugh, clearly getting a kick out of our sorry attempts at PDA. Nate waved his arms and pointed again. We turned.

Moss and Johnson pulled into the parking lot; cars pointed toward us where we stood next to the only two free spaces. Principal Moss got out. A sudden and violent tug at my shirt pulled me toward Alissa. Her lips, soft and spicy with pizza, locked with mine. My heart raced as I relaxed. As suddenly as it began, it was over. Alissa pulled away.

"Wha—" I gasped.

Alissa placed a finger to my lips and whispered. "Don't speak. Did you hear what they were talking about?"

My face grew hot. I licked my lips, embarrassed to admit it. "No. Not really."

"Of course not," Alissa grinned. "Let me recap anyway. Moss asked Johnson if she was absolutely sure that was the last of the boxes. She told him it was. He said it better be."

"That sounds like a threat," I said, feeling like I stated the obvious.

Alissa agreed. "Why are those boxes so important?"

Marcus

The door behind me chimed as it opened. I braced myself to be yanked toward Alissa.

Nate's voice came from behind me. "They just ordered a couple beers. They're going to be in there for a while."

Sagging with disappointment, I turned. Janice was by Nate's side.

Nate spoke to the three of us. "We can sit it out and go home or —"

"Stakeout," Janice said, raising an open palm toward Nate. They high-fived each other with a resounding slap.

"Fine," Alissa said. "But we can't stand around here looking all obvious when they come out."

Nate nodded. "I'd give each of you a dossier detailing your assignment, but we're operating impromptu at the moment."

We waited. Nate was really into all the spy stuff. As for me, I wanted to help Dad. But I had to admit, hearing the spy lingo did get me a little excited. Looking at the others, I could tell they were stoked, too.

"Marcus and I will hang out in my car," Nate said. He paused and looked at Alissa, who raised her hands in mock surrender.

"Don't look at me," she said. "For once, your plan works for me."

"Great!" Nate said. "Alissa, you and Janice will wait in your car. You'll follow Johnson while we follow Principal Moss. If they go in different directions, we'll be covered. Whatever happens, though, don't engage. This is an intel assignment, nothing more."

Something about this assignment seemed off, and not because it was impromptu. I felt like we were missing a big piece of the puzzle. One that had to do with the budget reports Alissa got from Principal Moss. Maybe the boxes in the cars would help fit the puzzle together. Getting to the boxes would be a different plan altogether. The best we could do was find out where they were taking the boxes.

Chapter Fourteen

Alissa

"This is so boring," Janice said. "Moss and Johnson have been in there for over an hour. Maybe we should just call it quits."

As I picked up my phone to text Marcus and tell him we were going to call it a night, Janice's phone buzzed. She stared at the screen.

"Guess what," Janice said as she typed a reply and spoke. "Nate says Moss is in the bathroom, and Johnson is on her way out."

As she said this, our target, Mrs. Johnson, opened the door to Nick's. We shrank in our seats, hoping she wouldn't look our way. In the middle of the parking lot, she stopped, pulled something out of her purse, then looked around.

Janice raised her phone up over the dashboard.

"What're you doing?" I whispered.

"Running surveillance," Janice said. "Someone's got to record this."

She had a point. As Johnson passed the rear of Moss' car, a dark blue Mercedes SUV, she knelt quickly and stuck something beneath the vehicle. While kneeling, she seemed to tighten her shoelaces. Then she stood and got into her car, a white BMW.

"What was that?" Janice whispered.

"I don't know," I said.

Janice watched the replay on her phone. "I feel like I just shot a clip for Riverdale."

"This isn't some murder mystery," I said. "None of our friends are dying off."

Janice glared at me for a moment. "Good look at keeping it real."

Johnson pulled her car out of the parking lot. We waited until we saw her take a left turn onto the road. I pulled my car out of the parking lot at a tip-toe's pace. When Johnson's car passed the light, I followed her.

We'd been following her for several blocks when my phone buzzed.

Janice grabbed my phone. "Uh-oh," she said.

"Something happen with Marcus and Nate?" I asked.

"No, a text from Bri," Janice said. She read, "Dad's freaking out. Marcus needs to get home."

Janice typed back.

"What're you saying?" I asked.

"She said he just got back from pizza delivery," Janice said.

"Why is she texting me and not Marcus?" I asked.

Janice shrugged. My phone chimed.

"Dad's not right," Janice read. "Okay, he's sitting down. He's —"

"Is she giving you a play-by-play?" I asked.

Janice typed back. "Alright. She says he's okay, but Marcus still should be back no later than 11. Sounds serious."

Not only that, I realized. But we'd be in a heap of trouble if the cops pulled us over after 11 pm. We were going to cut it awfully close. I imagined when 11 pm hit, I'd be pulled over right away as if a cop had been tailing me the entire time, ready to cherry-pick a ticket the second he could.

Up ahead, Johnson clicked on her left-hand blinker and pulled into a gated community, Deer Creek Run.

"We can't follow her in there," Janice said, setting my phone down. "That'll look way too obvious. But at least we know where she lives."

I nodded. "I heard this place is pretty pricey."

"It is," Janice said. She was looking at her phone. "Says here starting price is 1.2 million, and the community isn't even finished yet."

"That's insane," I said. "Johnson's an assistant principal. No way she's making that kind of money."

"Maybe her husband makes a lot of money," Janice offered.

A flash of light caught my eyes. I glanced in the rearview mirror.

The light flashed again, but this time it flashed red and blue. A siren blared.

"This sucks," Janice said.

I pulled over, making sure to place both of my hands on the steering wheel. No way the cop would get me for something else. The silence in the car was so thick, I could have been alone. Like me, Janice seemed to be holding her breath. She sank lower in an attempt to make herself invisible.

Through the side mirror, I saw the officer approaching. As the officer came closer, I noticed she was a woman. Once she was at the side of my car, I rolled down my window. I squinted when she shined her flashlight first on me, then on Janice. She cut the light off.

"I'm Officer Corcoran," she said without a single trace of emotion in her voice. "You girls are out late. But it's not quite 11 pm. Were you following anyone?"

I froze, wondering if Mrs. Johnson recognized us. Fortunately, Janice spoke up. Her voice cracked. "We're actually lost. I tried to get maps on my phone. But no reception."

Corcoran eyed Janice for a moment before turning her attention back on me. "Where you headed?" She asked.

"Home," I said. "We... we must have made a wrong turn somewhere. I get turned around in these housing developments when it gets too dark."

If she cared about my response, she didn't show it. Instead, she asked, "How long have you been driving?"

"Almost a year," I said.

The officer smiled. "That's good. License and registration."

The glovebox snapped open. Janice handed me the registration. I took it and dug around in the center console for my license. "Excuse me," I said to Officer Corcoran. "I need to unbuckle for a moment."

Corcoran took a step back. I unbuckled and twisted so I could get a better view. Janice turned on her phone's flashlight and illuminated the dark abyss of my car's center console. I rooted around coins and discarded papers until I found my license.

"Sorry," I said as I handed both the license and the registration to Corcoran. "It's my first car."

"Sit tight," Corcoran said. "I'll be back in a few."

"This isn't good," I said. "We should definitely contact the boys."

"Already on it," Janice said.

Janice's phone buzzed with a message. "Oh no," Janice said. "Moss has been run off the road."

"What? How?" I said, panic gripping my throat. "What about Marcus and Nate?"

Janice had no time to find out. Corcoran was back.

"You, girls, okay?" She asked. "Ms. Claude. This is your first time being pulled over, so it could be a little scary, especially for a sixteen-year-old. No need to worry, though. Your license won't be revoked. You'll need to follow me as I escort you home. Your parents will be expecting you."

With trembling hands, I replaced my license and registration. My license may not be legally revoked, but my parents will do it, I was sure of that. I turned on the car and followed Officer Corcoran. I was even more worried about Marcus and Nate. If Moss had been run off the road and they were witnesses, they'll have a lot more to concern themselves with than a single cop and worked-up-parents.

Chapter Fifteen

Marcus

"Bro," Nate said. "You think we should check it out?"

I was already out of the car. I didn't have to think twice about checking in on Moss. Whatever information he had on Dad could wait. Moss needed our help. His car, a dark blue Mercedes SUV, was rammed against a lamppost. Steam rose from the crunched hood. Moss hadn't exited yet.

"You coming?" I asked.

With deliberation, Nate got out of the car. This surprised me since he is usually the first to run into action.

"That car back there," Nate said. "Did you get a look at it?"

He was referring to the sedan that had run Moss' SUV off the road. The car was going way too fast for this winding road. Its driver couldn't even keep it in the lane. "To be honest," I said. "I could only tell you it was lighter in color. Maybe an older model. Like something made twenty years ago."

Nate pulled out his phone. "I'm calling the police."

As I approached the SUV, I was tempted to open the trunk and see what was in the boxes. But more pressing was seeing if Moss was okay. I knocked on the window, then peered inside when no one opened it.

Moss had his phone up to his ear like nothing had happened. I knocked again. This time he looked up and signaled with his index finger for me to wait a minute. I felt like I was interrupting some critical conference call. Maybe I was.

My phone buzzed. I pulled it out of my pocket to see a text from Alissa.

Alissa: *It's Janice. You need to get home ASAP. Don't worry about Moss.*

I stepped away from the SUV.

What's up? I texted back.

Janice: *Your dad. Bri's pretty freaked out. Check your messages.*

I did that and saw several messages from Bri that I had missed. To summarize, last night, the pizza shop let him go. He'd been drinking.

My eyes froze on the words *drinking*. In all my life, I'd never seen my dad drink anything other than water or an occasional soda. Since he'd been placed on administrative leave, it's like he'd been making up for the lost time. I thought him getting a job would slow him down. Clearly, it didn't.

The SUV opened, and Moss stepped out. My home life had to be put on hold because he looked simultaneously shaken up and pissed off.

"What!" He yelled. "You boys been following me?'

I took a step back and bumped into Nate.

"Actually," Nate said. "We weren't. We were headed to the park. It's a small town. Not surprising, we'd appear to be following you.

Good thing we were because we saw what happened."

Clearly unconvinced, Moss narrowed his eyes as if targeting the truth deep within our souls. Suddenly, his features softened into a slight smile.

"Well, you guys must've gotten a look at the vehicle," he said. "Police will be here in a moment. I just called them."

"We called them, too," Nate said.

Turning his back on us, Moss began to pace around his vehicle. Between the muttering and cursing, I got the feeling he wasn't happy about dealing with his insurance.

"I don't think he bought it," I whispered to Nate. "Got anything else planned?"

"Not a clue," Nate said. "I just know we'll need to stick around as witnesses."

"Hopefully, the police won't take too long," I said.

I handed Nate my phone. Taking it, he skimmed over the texts from Bri. Frowning, he gave me the phone. "Don't worry," Nate said. "I got your back. I've got some experience dealing with drunk dads. Besides, your dad's not an alcoholic or anything, is he?"

"Not that I know of," I said. I only had time to wonder where the question even came from when the police sirens wailed.

We, including Principal Moss, turned.

"You boys better have something good to tell them," Moss said.

"Jeez," Nate muttered. "Last time we try to help a guy in need."

"No, kidding," I said.

* * *

Police vehicles pulled up to the crash site. Immediately, officers badgered us with a bunch of questions that ranged from whether we'd been drinking to our rate of speed. They assumed we were the cause of the accident.

"Oh, no," Moss said, coming to our defense. "They witnessed the accident. Finish up with them quickly because they have to get home." He shot us the narrowed-eyed look he gave us before.

My phone buzzed again.

Janice: *See if you can check under the rear of the car.*

I texted back, *That'll be kind of hard to do. Why?*

Janice: *IDK. Johnson put something there.*

I showed the text to Nate. He nodded.

An officer approached us and introduced himself as Officer Robinson. "We understand you witnessed this accident," Robinson said.

"We didn't really see much," I began.

"But, man, what we did see was incredible!" Nate shouted. Suddenly, he darted into the street and took off down the road before the officer could stop him.

"You need to get back here!" Robinson called. He signaled for the other two officers who'd arrived a moment after him.

It was my turn to improvise. "It's okay. Nate gets this way when he's excited. Just wait."

At full speed, Nate ran around the bend in the road. As he did, he made engine noises in imitation of what I imagined to be the sedan we'd seen.

"Then Principal Moss did this! Nate yelled.

Nate swerved to the left, then to the right, bearing down on Moss' SUV in imitation of the vehicle. When he was six feet from the SUV he dove, feet first into the ground, like he was sliding into third base. When he came to a halt, he was almost, but not quite directly under the rear of the car.

"That's quite a show," Robinson said, taking several notes.

"Hey," Nate called. "What's this?"

Robinson stuffed his pen and pad into his pocket and pulled out his flashlight. Two other officers approached the vehicle. I followed. One of the officers knelt down. He pulled out a plastic bag and used it to grab a small rectangular box.

Nate's eyes widened when he saw what it was. Without a word, the officer approached Moss and asked him about the device. Moss began to pace back and forth, clearly agitated.

"I've never seen that in my life," Moss said, grabbing his phone. "Excuse me." With his back toward us, he leaned against the SUV.

"Gentlemen," Robinson said as he turned to us. "You've both been a help tonight. Here's my card if you think of anything else. You be safe as you head home."

Returning to Nate's Jeep, we each pocketed the cards the officer gave us. Nate keyed the ignition and pulled the Jeep onto the road. A mile down the road, Nate finally spoke.

"Bro!" Nate exclaimed. "He had a tracking device on his SUV."

"That's insane," I said. "Why would Johnson put that on his vehicle?"

Nate glanced at me and furrowed his brow. "Maybe it has something to do with the ticket booth."

"If that's the case," I said, adding a pause as I carefully considered my next words. "Johnson had been using the ticket booth as some kind of hiding place."

Nate muttered, "Or your dad was."

Marcus

I glared at Nate, who kept his eyes on the road, careful to avoid eye-contact with me. I had to admit, his speculation wasn't far-fetched. "We need more evidence," I said at last. "To clear his name, to put this puzzle together. To... Did you get a look at that thing attached to Moss' SUV? Was it pretty high tech?'

"Nah," Nate said. "In fact, I was looking to get one myself from Amazon. About fifty bucks."

"Still," I said. "Why would Johnson be tracking him *if* she's working with him?"

"That's what we're going to have to find out," Nate said. "But I'm pretty sure it has something to do with those boxes."

* * *

As Nate drove me home, we both racked our brains, trying to see the missing piece in a sea of circumstantial evidence. When we finally pulled up to my house, a single police car with flashing lights was parked out front. When I got out of the Jeep, I heard my dad cursing.

"Marcus," he shouted. "Get in right now. It's way past eleven pm."

As I walked up the sidewalk to my porch, I caught a glimpse of Alissa. Brow furrowed, she stood on her porch, watching me. She thumbed the air in front of her as if she was holding her phone. We'd definitely be on text tonight. Or, even better, we'd meet outside after everyone had gone to sleep.

"What have you boys been up to?" Dad yelled. "Why am I getting calls about you following the principal?'

"We weren't," I said. I climbed out of the Jeep.

"Do you need me to stick around?" Nate asked.

Dad waved him off. "It's already late. You drive safe.

Nate gave me a nod and drove off.

Before I spoke again, I attempted to formulate an argument. If Dad knew what we were up to, he would shut down our operation. On top of that, he'd be permanently out of a job.

Dad sighed. "Sit down, son."

I sat on the stoop.

"You're trying to help," he said as he paced. "I get that. But there's no need to get yourself in trouble." He stopped and looked directly at me. "Marcus, you've got a scholarship to worry about and—"

"It won't be there if you're not leading the athletics department," I said as I interrupted him.

"It also won't be there if you don't stay in your lane," Dad said. "Who do you guys think you are? The Hardy Boys?"

I shrank back. Coming from Dad, our little investigation sounded kind of stupid. Four kids trying to solve a mystery, they've concocted out of thin air. Good thing we didn't have a talking dog with us.

"Dad," I said. "We're just trying to help. You know, speed up the process."

Dad looked at me for a moment. He placed both of his hands against the back of his neck, giving himself a massage. He closed his eyes.

"Son," Dad said. "It's going to take a long time. There's a lot of paperwork they'll have to go through."

"Do you even know where your records are?" I asked.

"Boxed up and in my office," Dad said. "Why?"

I stood with a sudden realization. "Good night, Dad."

I neither had the heart, nor the evidence to tell him that those boxes were no longer in his office.

* * *

I plopped down on my bed and looked at my phone. There were several texts from Alissa.

Alissa: *Babe. I'm worried. Text me back. Okay*

Me: *Hey. I'm okay.*

Animated dots popped up beneath my text. I wasn't sure what to make of Alissa's use of *babe*. But my mind went back to our... her kissing me. Whoa! I wanted to believe our relationship was at the pet name stage, but I was pretty sure she had been acting in the moment.

My phone buzzed.

Alissa: *What's up? Is your dad fired from the pizza gig? What about that thing we saw?*

Me: *He's good. Just worried. Cheap tracking device. Boxes MIGHT contain dad's records.*

Alissa: *We need to get into his office.*

I thought back to the budget reports Alissa had gotten from Principal Moss. Dad would have to see those. Maybe he could check them with his own. But if his records were gone, he'd be toast.

Me: *Tomorrow. Nate and I will figure out how to get in.*

Alissa: *Just be careful. Maybe Janice and I can create a distraction.*

That was a good idea, I realized. But it needed a little bit more planning than a moment's notice.

Me: *I'll let you know about tomorrow. G' night.*

I set my phone down without waiting for her to respond. I laid back down, but my muscles were nervous knots of energy as I tossed and turned most of the night. No way getting my dad's files would be easy... if they were even there.

Chapter Sixteen

Marcus

The next afternoon, the four of us were standing just outside of the cafeteria. Two hundred feet down the hall were the athletic offices.

"You sure about this?" Alissa asked.

I nodded. "Just in case something goes wrong, create a diversion."

"We'll do more than create a diversion," Janice said. She and Nate exchanged a look of mischief. I looked at Alissa.

"Don't worry about it," Alissa said.

"Okay," I said. "See you soon."

Nate and I ducked into a crowded hallway. Freshman kids were milling about by their lockers, reluctant to get to their next class. We were on our lunch block and taking full advantage of the fact that freshman lockers were located in the athletic wing of the building.

If we were caught in this hallway, we determined we would play it cool and say we were signing up for an intramural sport. Those were open to everyone. We rounded down another corner, past the gymnasium, and finally, a dusty, dark corner of the building where, hanging from the ceiling, a single placard read *Athletic Director*.

The sign seemed so underwhelming. I wished it at least mentioned Dad's name, especially since he led the high school athletic department to many regional and national championships in multiple sports. The hallway we turned down served as proof of Dad's accomplishments. Glass cases, housing trophies dating back more than twenty years, lined the walls. The most recent ones were housed near the front office. Nate and I tiptoed our way down the hallway. The fluorescent lights above us flickered. A screech echoing off the cinder block walls caused us to pause and hold our breaths.

We breathed when we heard the screech again. It was followed by the clang of metal. We were near the weight room. Dunbar, my dad's fill-in, fell right into Dad's routine of working out at this time of day. It seemed Dunbar focused most of his efforts in the weight room. Though his workouts were typically an hour-long, we'd have to execute this operation quickly and quietly in the event he decided to cut his routine short.

"Bro," Nate whispered. "You keep a lookout while I jimmy the lock."

He pulled out a lock-picking kit from his cargo shorts and crouched at the door handle. I kept my guard up, swiveling to make sure no one was coming from either direction.

The door clicked open. Nate slipped in and turned on the flashlight end of his tactical pen. When I followed in after him, I shut and locked the door, then flipped on the light. We stood in a small office. It was enough room for a desk, two filing cabinets, a closet, a wheeled office chair, and stacks of file boxes. Only, where the file boxes should have been, the carpeted floor was a brilliant light blue, compared to the rest of the carpet aged by years of ground-in dirt.

Nate saw this too. "See. I told you Moss and Johnson were up to something."

He pulled a file cabinet open and began to rummage through some papers. I did the same.

I knew we were more than breaking a few school rules by being in this office and going through file cabinets. I was definitely invading Dad's privacy and the privacy of the many student-athlete files I came across. But that was only secondary. I wasn't even looking at the names or their records.

Nate slammed a file drawer shut. "You find anything yet?"

"Nothing," I answered. I turned to Nate. "I was wondering what—"

He put a finger to his mouth. The universal sign for *shut-your-mouth-and-listen.* Muffled voices, coupled with footsteps in the hallway, approached the door. We both slid into the closet as keys jingled. The door opened. Two people walked in.

"Who left this light on?" A woman's voice spoke.

"I don't know, ma'am." A man's voice replied.

"You find out which one of your people were in here last," the woman said.

"Yes, ma'am," the man said.

The door creaked as if it was being opened or closed. I couldn't tell. But I got the feeling that someone was leaving the room and hesitated a moment at the doorway.

The woman said, "Walter. I don't need to remind you how important it is that nothing of Mr. Kahale's administration in this department is left behind."

I wondered what she meant by that. It sounded pretty final. As though Dad's leave of absence wasn't a temporary thing that would eventually blow over when the union, or whoever, went through all of his files.

Metal drawers creaked with friction as they slid open, then shut again. I couldn't begin to imagine how long Mr. Walter, the head custodian in our school, would take in this office. It was small, so it couldn't take too long. Not only that, it was pretty clear they already did an excellent job of cleaning the place out.

Padded footsteps and the jingle of keys hanging on a belt loop approached the closet.

The knob turned.

My heart thumped.

A radio beeped.

I held my breath.

A staticky female voice spoke, "Spill clean-up needed in the cafe hallway."

"10-4," Mr. Walter said. "On my way."

The lights flipped off, the door swung shut, and the click of the key tumblers indicated the finality of Nate and I being alone once again in this room.

A minute felt like ten in the silent waiting. I wondered if the spill clean-up had anything to do with the little diversion Janice and Alissa had planned.

Papers rustled beside me as Nate moved around. He turned his flashlight on.

"Look at this," he whispered.

He was sitting on what looked like a heap of file boxes. A few papers looked like financial reports, but I couldn't tell from where I was sitting. Not to mention, I was not the one with the flashlight.

"Hold this," Nate said. I took the flashlight from him while he stood.

The closet was beginning to get way too cramped. "If your butt gets any closer to my face," I said, "I'm outta here."

Nate chuckled. "Coast should be clear. Turn the office light on."

I stood and gladly exited the closet. Nate was already in the middle of the room with a box when I turned the light on.

"Ah, man. Check these out," Nate said. He was flipping through some papers he'd found.

I knelt and pulled out a few sheets. Each one was dated. From what I could tell, Dad had indiscriminately dropped into the box various receipts attached to paid invoices, along with signed deposit slips. There wasn't any more organization to it than that. I guess he didn't intend to ever look at these again. Boy, he was going to be in for a huge surprise. I checked the date of the box. September 2016.

"What're the other boxes labeled?" I asked.

Nate set down a handful of papers and peeked into the closet. "Two are labeled as 1995. Another is labeled as 2010. Strange system of organization your dad has."

I looked at the box at my feet. "Too bad we can't take this box, and the one labeled 2010. 1995 is way too old. My dad didn't start his position here until 2001."

Nate plopped himself in the wheelie chair and began to slowly spin. "What if that box was all the way at the bottom of the closet for a reason?" He asked.

"I don't know," I said. I glanced at the office door. "We should probably get out of here soon, though. Mr. Walter is bound to come back soon."

"You're right," he said. "Let's grab a sampling of papers from each file box."

I smiled and nodded. "I see where you're going with this. Gonna check these over with the budget sheets we got from Principal Moss."

Nate grinned. "Look at you, Nancy Drew."

We bumped fists, then continued to gather evidence. I held onto hope that we could take at least one piece of useful evidence to my dad. Maybe he'd look at the budget sheets from Moss, look at the records he kept, and see something was seriously wrong, not with his own records, but with Moss' records.

"You good?" Nate asked.

His cargo shorts were stuffed with rolled sheets of paper. It looked super suspicious. But no more than I felt. Placing my hands behind my back, I adjusted the paper-filled folder tucked between the small of my back and my pants.

"Good as I'll ever be," I said. "Let's get out of here."

Nate hit the lights and opened the office door. I followed as he slipped out into the hallway. Standing there, we listened for the screeching and clanging of metal from the weight room. It never came.

"Dunbar's done working out," I whispered.

Nate nodded. I wasn't keeping track, but I was pretty sure our lunch block was almost, if not definitely, over. Nate picked up the pace; I matched his. Suddenly, Dunbar rounded the corner. Nate grabbed me and did an about-face. I realized he was almost as shocked to see Dunbar as I was.

"Gentlemen," Dunbar called.

We turned around. From the corner of my eye, I saw Nate shielding his surprise with a blank, emotionless face. Poker masters would be proud.

"Yes," I said. There was a slight shaking in my voice.

Dunbar held out a stiff hand. I took it. His grasp on my own hand was too firm and his narrowed eyes too searching.

He grinned. "I saw you coming down earlier. Something I can help you two with?"

I shook my head and pulled my hand away. He let go as I said, "Ummm... looking to sign up for intramurals."

"You're already pretty deep in cross country," he said.

"It's for me," Nate said.

Dunbar swiveled toward him. "A techie signing up for sports. That's a new one."

"Not really," Nate said.

"So," I said. "The sign-up sheets?"

"Back toward the cafeteria. Hang left at the corner."

"Thanks," Nate and I said. We beelined it toward the cafe.

"Marcus," Dunbar called.

We froze. A lump formed in my throat. I turned slowly.

"Yes, sir?"

"How's your father holding up?"

"He's good," I lied. "Thanks." I turned to leave.

"I meant to tell you, great run last week." Dunbar shot me a thumbs up. "You boys stay out of trouble."

This time, we got out of there as fast as we could. When we rounded the corner, Alissa and Janice were waiting for us. Lunch was still going on, so they didn't look entirely out of place.

"Did you get what you needed?" Alissa asked.

Nate patted his pockets. "Yup. Thanks for the save."

Janice winked. "Somebody needed to cry over spilled milk."

I didn't need to ask. "We should probably get moving before Dunbar comes around again."

"We saw him go down," Alissa said. "Did he suspect anything?"

"Maybe," Nate said as he nudged me. "Marcus' nervous energy was impossible to miss."

"Good thing it was Dunbar and not Moss," I said. "Pretty sure things would've gone down a lot differently."

"True story," Nate said. "We're running into him way too much."

"Guys," Janice said. "We should *definitely* get going because Moss is headed toward the cafeteria right now."

We parted ways. I couldn't believe Dunbar just let us go. Either one of two things were true — he was a big, lazy dummy, or that's a front, and he's completely aware of everything that is going on. I tended toward the later. There was something about his line of questioning that made me feel like he'd been baiting me. I just couldn't tell whether I'd passed his little test.

Chapter Seventeen

Alissa

That evening we all gathered in Marcus' bedroom where Janice sat cross-legged on the floor, with her laptop open while she scanned a spreadsheet. Meanwhile, Marcus and I sorted through stacks of paper he and Nate managed to steal from his dad's office.

Without looking up from her work, Janice demanded another document faster than Marcus and I could sort through them. Mr. Kahale's documents were a hot mess: inventories with single jagged staples and receipts for supplies or services without a matching invoice.

"I'll trade you a receipt for one hundred jockstraps for your invoice for towels," Marcus said.

I felt like I was playing some lame card game. "Here," I said as I spotted the invoice and handed it to Marcus. He stapled his together, gave me the stapler, and I did the same. These we handed to Janice.

"Thanks," Janice said and turned to the computer. "You know, Marcus. This would go a lot easier if your dad was more organized."

"Tell me about," Marcus said. "This is terrible."

"You know what else is terrible?" I asked. I eyed Nate. He was hunched over the desk, his back to us.

"You know, Alissa," Nate said. "I can feel your eyes boring into me."

Marcus laughed. I slapped him lightly with some papers. "Well, Nathan, if you're gonna play quartermaster in this operation, I sure hope you've got something good we'll be able to use."

"Once we have a plan," he said. "I'll think of something. Right now, I'm getting some supplies together for the field. Nothing too 007, but definitely practical items."

I smirked. I'd already seen Marcus' tactical pen, but I still didn't know what it did. "Alright, M," I said to Marcus. "I guess that leaves you. What've you got for us?"

Janice and Nate turned from their work, giving Marcus their full attention. Face flushed, Marcus shrank back.

I sat next to him and nudged him. "Go ahead, babe. You've got this."

Though I could tell he wasn't feeling one hundred percent ready, I also knew he could give us something to go on. I'd seen what he could do, especially with a supportive team like us behind him.

Marcus cleared his throat. "So far, we've got nothing more than fifty or sixty pieces of paper. Not much to go on, I admit."

Marcus stood and began to pace the room. When he passed the stacks of paper, he began to flip through them. I knew he was buying time. I'd do the same.

"Here's what we know," Marcus continued. "Moss' car had some tracking device that Johnson most likely planted. Those alleged boxes may, or may not be from Dad's office—"

"But," Nate interrupted. "They most likely are because—

Marcus held up a hand. "Maybe, or maybe Dad's lawyers got the boxes. I need to confirm that somehow without letting on what we're up to. He'd definitely tell us to back off, or worse. I'm sure of that."

"True," I said. "Remember, also, the reports Moss gave us. Janice, did you find anything that matched or raised a red flag?"

Janice shook her head. "I'm not sure. Maybe? Look at this."

She got up and opened her laptop out on the bed. We gathered around it. Next to the laptop, she laid out one of the reports Moss had given to us.

"I was thinking," Janice said. "These budgets are all from this school year. So, spending from previous school years should be mostly the same, right?"

A knock came at the door. Janice closed her laptop. Marcus went to the door while the three of us grabbed handfuls of paper and laid them upside down. The door opened to Mr. Kahale standing in the doorway.

"Hey, kids," he said. "How's the school project coming along?"

"Good," we said.

He eyed us. "Care to share?"

Somehow, I realized, he seemed more put together today. Like he was happier, but I was pretty sure it had nothing to do with the new light blue pizza uniform with the bright red logo.

"We're good," Marcus said. "Just an accounting project."

Mr. Kahale raised an eyebrow. "I didn't think you'd be taking that this year."

"I changed my schedule," Marcus said. Though he was lying, his voice was steady, projecting confidence.

"That's great," Mr. Kahale said. "When I get back to work, you'll be able to help sort out the papers."

He sounded super hopeful. I hoped he had the boxes because that would definitely make all this sneaking about completely unnecessary.

"You're coming back then," Marcus said. "Because Mr. Dunbar is not—"

"Did you say, Dunbar?" Mr. Kahale interrupted. "He can't even lead a heard of mice to cheese."

Janice snorted. Mr. Kahale glanced at her, smiled, and returned his attention back to

Marcus. "Marcus, I wanted to talk to you about some things before I head out. Do you three mind lending him for a few minutes?"

"It's cool," I said.

As they left, Marcus stole a glance over his shoulder and shrugged. He was as surprised by this interruption as we were.

"What's that about?" Nate asked.

"No idea," I said. "While Marcus is gone, why don't we see if we can sort out more of this paperwork. And Nate," I said just as he was sitting down. "You're helping this time."

Nate sighed. "Fine. I was just about finished with your gear anyway."

I glanced at the desk and saw three piles of dark objects. I recognized a small flashlight in each pile, then a few dark, shiny items I couldn't identify. "Exactly what are we doing with those anyway?"

"As I was saying," Janice said as she popped open the computer and straightened up the papers. "These old budget reports Marcus and Nate grabbed. There's not a category for overtime. The administrative costs also seemed to have nearly doubled. I'm not sure if it has anything to do with inflation, but here." She handed me the 2010 report. "I compared this to this year's report. Credit card processing wasn't on the 2010 report either. But that definitely doesn't account for the increase."

Nate leaned in to get a better look. "Most people, when they go to games, also still pay with cash. So, it's tough to tell from our end if they've been fooling with the books."

There was a slight drop in Janice's head as she spoke. "Overtime then?"

"Same," I said. "Seems weird the school would suddenly have overtime. But I also think about those discretionary funds Moss told us about. Maybe there's something there."

As Janice toggled to another spreadsheet, Nate plopped back in his seat. He turned and began to fiddle with some of the gadgets. I looked over his shoulder and recognized the tactical pen, the multi-tool, and the pick-kit. "Do we really need those things as well?"

I caught a twitch in Nate's eye when he turned toward me. He opened his mouth to speak, but the door opened.

With furrowed a brow, Marcus walked in, shut the door behind him, and took a seat at the edge of his bed. "Do you guys remember those boxes Moss and Johnson were carrying out? Dad's lawyers went looking for them. They're gone."

Nate stood up and shouted. "I knew it! But," he lowered his voice, "Why are they trying to sabotage him?"

"Only one way to find out," Marcus said. "Time to execute the plan!"

The boy's fist-bumped.

"Hold up," I said. They frowned, like I was some sort of buzzkill, which I guess I was. "You better get sharing because I'm none too happy about being kept in the dark."

"Me neither," Janice said. She turned to me. "Let's make them talk, Lis."

Marcus and Nate both looked sheepishly at each other, but I could still see the mischief in both of their eyes.

"Spill it, boy!" I said. "Then we'll consider forgiving you *and* going along with your plan."

Marcus and Nate talked animatedly, starting and finishing each other's sentences.

"We're going to use my stealth," Nate said.

"And my speed and my gift of quiet observation," Marcus added.

"And Janice's dramatic skills," Nate added. "Along with Lis'..."

Nate glanced at Marcus. Marcus' eyes shifted from him to me.

I crossed my arms. "Lis' what?"

Nate took a purposeful step back. "Badassness," he added.

Alissa

I scowled. "For what, exactly?"

"To break into Principal Moss' office and find the reports my dad did submit," Marcus offered.

"Guys," I said. "That is a dumb idea... and what's this with my badassness? What does that even mean?"

Marcus sat. "See. I told you she wouldn't like it."

"Hold up," Nate said. "Let's go over the fine details."

As they did, I sat while my patience waned. But, in the end, it wasn't the worst plan. Janice and I would create another diversion while Marcus and Nate broke into Principal Moss' office to, hopefully, find the files they were looking for. I only wondered how we'd pull it off without getting caught and losing our chances at scholarships.

Chapter Eighteen

Alissa

We decided to execute this plan as quickly as possible. As in, the very next day. Seconds after the bell rang at the end of the day, the four of us met at the bus entrance.

"You guys —" Marcus began.

Janice cut him off, "Girls."

Nate rolled his eyes.

"What?" Janice said. "Got a problem with being gender specific?"

Heat rose to my neck.

"Fine," Marcus said. "Alissa and Janice. Are you two ready?"

We nodded. "As ready as we can be," I said, though I wasn't so sure how this whole diversion thing was going to work. We stood at the bus entrance. Kids pushed past us, while the athletes gathered in the cafe for a pre-practice after school meal. It was a perfect time, I conceded, to create a diversion. I just didn't think Janice pretending to hyperventilate would work... even with her talents in acting.

"Ready, Lis?" Janice grabbed my arm and led me away.

I shot Marcus a glance. He returned it with a shrug and a crooked smile.

"Good luck," Marcus said.

"Thanks... uh... you, too." I added. What he and Nate intended was far worse and could result in expulsion from school if they were caught.

Janice's cheery voice broke through my reservations. "You ready for this?" she asked with a big grin.

"Just a sec," I answered, checking the time. "Moss should be coming around the corner at any moment."

"In the meantime," Janice said. "I've got to go to the bathroom."

"Wait—" I said. But Janice was already gone, leaving me to watch as Moss, right on schedule, approached the bus entrance. He shooed away the last of the stragglers to go home and coaxed a group of athletes, boys and girls, into the cafeteria. Practice didn't start for another ten minutes, so I knew we were good. I could see Marcus in the distance, peaking around the corner. He was supposed to be the lookout. We exchanged a thumbs up. Nate was probably already in the office.

Just then, I heard Janice scream as the sounds of gushing water came from the bathroom. I darted to the bathroom door, but froze when I heard someone shout, "What's going on?"

I did an about-face and cringed. Principal Moss was right there within arm's reach.

"Principal Moss!" I exclaimed.

An alarm rang before I had time to even make an excuse. Moss pushed past me without giving me a second glance.

Alissa

Moss reappeared. "You," he said. "Call 9-1-1. There's a girl in here knocked out, and the sprinkler system is on."

Then, he disappeared into the girl's bathroom. Before I could react, Mrs. Johnson and another administrator came around the corner where, moments before, Marcus had been standing.

My fingers shook as I dialed one digit, then the next. My mind fought for control over my body. Fighting against the urge to run into the bathroom and check in on Janice, I waited. An operator came on.

"What's your emergency?" the 9-1-1 operated asked.

"There's a girl," I said. "She's knocked out in the bathroom."

"Can you describe her condition?" The operator asked.

"Yeah... hold on a sec." I stepped into the bathroom. Water sprayed from the ceiling.

"Excuse me," Mrs. Johnson said. Without waiting for me to move, she blew by me and hovered over Principal Moss.

As I took in the scene before me, I did my best to describe it to the 9-1-1 operator.

Besides Moss, Janice was sprawled out on the floor. A trickle of blood seeped from her forehead. Moss knelt next to Janice as water soaked through his suit.

"She's hit her head pretty hard, I think." Principal Moss said.

Johnson grabbed some towels, knelt, and began to dab Janice's forehead. She lightly slapped Janice's face, coaxing her to wake up.

"She doesn't seem to be responsive," I added.

The 9-1-1 operator buzzed some instructions into my ear. "An ambulance is on the way," I shouted.

Johnson stood. "Nice work. I'll go to meet it. You stay here."

I nodded and stayed on the line.

"Stay awake," Principal Moss shouted. Janice's eyelids flickered. Moss let out a sigh. "Good job. Can you get up? We've got to get out of here."

Unsteadily, Janice attempted to rise, stealing a glance at me. Though she was clearly disoriented, I could've sworn she wore a smirk on her face.

"EMTs should be there in five," the 9-1-1 operator said. "Stay with me, okay?"

"Okay," I said, relaying what was happening as Mr. Walter, followed by two other members of the custodial staff, pushed past me.

"Cut off the mainline and get some buckets and mops," Mr. Walter said to his team. The custodians left. A moment later, the rush of water ceased, and Janice propped herself against the wall. Dunbar and the JV soccer coach, Mrs. Moreau, arrived on the scene.

"Great. Excellent," Principal Moss said, rising. "Alissa, Janice is your friend, right? Stay with her a moment. I've got to change. When the paramedics come, I need you to stay put and tell me everything that happened. Okay? You can do that, right?"

I nodded.

But, in my head, I was thinking, *Janice, what the hell did you do?*

Chapter Nineteen

Marcus

A minute after Alissa flashed me a thumbs up, I heard Principal Moss shout, "What's going on!"

I glanced at Nate.

He shrugged, "I guess that's our diversion."

He popped Principal Moss' office door open.

Marcus

When the door latched shut, I was left alone for seconds before an alarm went off. Athletes began to scurry in a swarm of confusion. Johnson and another administrator came rushing out of the main office. I braced myself against the wall as they passed by, radios in their hands.

I had no idea what was going on. Janice was supposed to create a diversion, not cause mass hysteria among the administrative staff. Custodians appeared. Compared to the administrators who'd just passed by, these three seemed to lumber down the hall.

When they passed me, I glanced around the corner again. Alissa was pacing. Her cell was to her ear. I tried to get her attention, but she didn't see me. Instead, she darted into the bathroom. Right behind her was Mrs. Johnson. The other assistant principal stayed outside, shouting at kids and trying to corral them away from the entrance.

I hid behind the corner again. With the action happening by the girls' bathroom, this hallway remained pretty quiet. I took my cell phone out and texted Nate, *What's going on?*

He didn't give a response. I did the same for Alissa. *I'm over here*, I texted. *What's happening?*

Then I realized she was still be on the phone. As sirens wailed in the distance, my heart seemed to skip a beat. Somehow, Janice, who was supposed to faint, made this diversion into something completely different. I wondered if Nate and Janice had some secret meeting last night and decided upon some even crazier scheme. But that thought passed. Nate would've wanted something far less conspicuous.

Between Moss' office door and the corner of the hallway, I paced until I froze. Between a gap in a small crowd of athletes, I caught a glimpse of a couple of EMTs rolling in a gurney. When they were out of sight, I stared once again at the backs of some athletes.

"Everyone get to practice!" shouted an administrator.

The crowd dissipated, but not enough to allow a clear line of sight to the bathroom as the gurney rolled out. It looked like Janice was on it. She was supposed to pretend to pass out. I wondered what she did instead. Perhaps she misjudged her fall and hit her head on the floor.

Suddenly, I got a partial answer as the remaining athletes went their separate way. Principal Moss, suit soaked to the skin, hustled in my direction. I knew where he was headed next. I hid behind the corner again and texted Nate.

Marcus

He's coming.

No response. I was about to text him again when my phone chimed.

Stall him, Nate's text read.

I turned on my heals and bumped right into Principal Moss.

Chapter Twenty

Alissa

About a thousand things ran through my head as they carted Janice, soaking wet and semi-conscious, out of the bathroom. I wondered whether she suddenly decided to pretend to play at being Simone Biles and do backflips from the bathroom sink.

As the EMTs passed with the gurney, I didn't wait to be told what to do next. Once Moss, dripping water all over the place, squeaked on past me, I was outta there. The boys would have to figure things out on their own, especially if they got caught. I was already guilty by association. Having someone's back can only go so far. We all had something to lose — potential scholarships, to name just one if we got caught — but, at the moment, I needed to make sure my best friend, Janice, was okay.

In a sec, I was out in my car. When the ambulance pulled out of the parking lot, I hit the gas and followed on the main road. For a hot second, I thought about Marcus and Nate. But that second cooled. It should've been Marcus who'd created the diversion, not Janice. Now, I was following an ambulance carting Janice to the hospital for, worst-case scenario, a concussion. I decided I would let both boys know how dumb this whole thing was.

I pulled up to the hospital parking just as Mrs. Johnson, trailing behind the EMTs pushing the gurney, disappeared beyond the sliding glass door. I shut my car off, slammed the door, and sprinted in just behind them. Janice's parents were in the lobby.

"Mrs. Kane," I called. She spun. She had the same dark curls and freckles that Janice had. Her eyes, red and puffy with tears, took a second to register me.

"Alissa," she said.

I ran to her and suddenly found myself crying into her shoulder. She took a step back and searched my eyes.

"What happened?" She asked.

"I... don't know," I said. I was ninety percent confident in that truth. "One moment she tells me she's going to the bathroom. The next, I hear her scream followed by a loud crash. Then rushing water."

It was Johnson's turn to spin on me. "Any idea what she was doing in there?"

This, I knew, I couldn't lie about. I had an idea, and that idea brought me back to Marcus, and Nate in Moss' office. By this time, they were gone or caught.

"It all happened so fast," I said, stalling as I thought of something that wouldn't incriminate me or get the others in trouble. "I... can I just see her?"

Johnson looked at Janice's parents. They nodded.

"Well," Mrs. Johnson said. "When you're ready, come find me. There's a lot that just doesn't make sense, and we think you're our best bet at discovering the truth."

I let those words sink in. "I'll see you tomorrow." Though, I had no idea what I would tell her. Honesty, they say, is always the best policy. But I didn't think that applied here. I believed we were definitely on to something. So, there was no way we could be totally up front without revealing what we were up to. As I walked into Janice's room, I resolved, no matter what, I'd not turn on my friends.

Chapter Twenty-One

Marcus

I thought my own eyes would pop out onto the floor. Moss stood before me, sopping wet and severely agitated. My mind raced, thinking of a way to stall him.

"Hey," Principal Moss," I said shakily. "Can I ask you something?"

Principal Moss brushed past me. "Whatever is so important will have to wait. If you'd notice, there's an emergency, and I'm soaked."

I took a step back. "I'll wait here then."

Moss fumbled with his keys while I shot Nate a text. No response.

"Principal Moss, sir," I said. "I know you're super busy."

Turning, he glared at me while he kept his hand on the doorknob. "What is it?"

"Next week's cross-country meet," I blurted out. "Can you at least —"

"Listen," He said. "We're in the middle of an emergency here. Now, move over."

He meant business, and I was out of time. Moss pushed open the door. He paused.

"That's funny," he said. "I thought I locked this."

"Maybe in your rush —"

Moss' heavy sigh cut me off. "Marcus. I'll give you five minutes, okay?"

"I don't need any more than three," I said and followed him inside.

A warm, light breeze flowed through the window. Principal Moss sat. With a furrowed brow, he stared at his desk on which sat his laptop and a printer that blinked, signally it was out of paper. He seemed unaware that the window was even open. Obviously, I was not. Clearly, Nate had made it out, leaving the office completely spotless. I only hoped he'd found the files we needed. Principal Moss glanced behind him at the filing cabinet Alissa and Janice had told us about.

I swallowed a lump forming in my throat. "Is everything okay, sir?"

Ignoring my question, he asked, "What is it, Marcus?"

I sensed a clear edge in his voice. I had to make it quick. "The team's been talking, so have the parents. They've agreed to fund the trip, if..."

My voice trailed off when I saw Principal Moss staring at the window. He sat back. "What trip is this?"

"Listen," I said. "I just remembered I have to pick up my sister from school. Can we schedule a meeting?'

Moss narrowed his eyes and crossed his arms. I shifted my weight from one foot to the other. I had to get out of there, and I hoped I wasn't looking too suspicious.

"I didn't thank you," he said. "You and Nate were really quick on the scene of the hit and run I had."

"Must've been providence," I said. "Did the police ever catch the guy who ran you off the road?"

Moss shook his head. "Nate's tip was... interesting."

"Yeah," I said, then jolted my hand as if I'd gotten a text. "So, uh, Bri is getting a little anxious because..."

"Go ahead," Moss said. "Schedule something with my secretary, Mrs. Heinemann."

"Thanks," I said. As I shut the office door, I heard Moss mumbling about everything being really off today.

I couldn't agree with him more.

Chapter Twenty-Two

Alissa

I sat in the hospital waiting room thumbing through a magazine because neither of the boys was answering their texts or calls. Janice hadn't woken up. Not the first time her parents walked into her room, and not the tenth time when her father walked out to get another coffee. I could totally relate.

I was feeling it, too. The anxiety. It was like my mom had passed it on to me an hour ago when I'd called to let her know where I was. She insisted on coming over. I matched her insistence with my own.

"Seriously, mom," I said. "I'm okay. You and dad can stay home."

"You sure, honey," my mother said. Her voice was shaky. In the background, I heard my father calling to her, "Let's go."

"Please tell dad I'm in good hands. The Kanes are here. I'll let you know how she's doing when I get home."

"Richard," my mom called. "Put the keys away. The Kanes are with her."

I heard the keys jingle and land on the table right beside the door. I imagined my father trudging off as he called, "Joshana! If she's not home in an hour, we're picking her up."

My mom's voice came through the receiver, "You hear —"

"I did," I said. "Doc said Janice'll be waking up any minute. Probably just a minor concussion. Nothing to worry about."

My mother sucked in a deep breath, "Do you know what happened?"

I thought back to the rushing waters. It was loud, but not so much that I didn't hear Janice yell. I wondered if she'd climbed onto the sink.

"I don't know," I said. "I love you, mom."

I sighed as I locked the screen of my phone and stuffed it into my pocket. I hadn't lied. It's also not like I knew exactly what happened.

As I grabbed another magazine, Doc came toward Janice's room just as her dad returned with another cup of coffee. Her mom stepped out. Deep wrinkles in their foreheads told me the conversation was serious. Mrs. Kane looked like she was about to cry, and Mr. Kane nodded his head, slowly at first. Then the three of them stepped into Janice's room.

For a minute, I waited and took the time to check my phone. I'd already blown Marcus' phone up with multiple texts. I wanted to believe Marcus and Nate had made it out of the building without getting caught. Somehow, though, I felt like our actions needed a punishment. After all, we did some foolish things today that got Janice hurt. I only hoped she'd recover and be back to her usual, chipper self.

I stood and beelined it toward her room, ready to tell all.

"Alissa," Marcus' voice called from behind me. I spun. From down the corridor, he and

Nate strolled toward me. As they approached, their furrowed brows and downcast eyes told me they'd gotten my texts and my calls.

Anger and relief bubbled up inside me. "Geez, Marcus! Where've you guys been?"

Marcus cringed. "Sorry. Nate captured some —"

"How's Janice?" Nate asked, interrupting Marcus' explanation.

"Still out," I said. "But she'll be okay."

Creases in Nate's brows seemed to vanish as he took a deep breath and exhaled slowly. "Have you been to see her?"

Every part of me wanted to scream. I'd sent the boys tons of updates, but I gritted my teeth. "If you'd checked your texts and answered my calls, you'd know."

Nate took a step back. "Yeah. About that. I was in hiding and —"

"I was trying to find him," Marcus interrupted. "Then he showed me some pretty damaging evidence."

I crossed my arms. "And you couldn't have picked up a phone or acknowledged a text."

The boys gave me a blank stare. I imagined I looked about the same when my parents caught me doing something I wasn't supposed to be doing. I eased up.

"Sorry, guys," I said. "All of this is just getting out of hand."

"Lis," Mrs. Kane called.

I turned, thankful for the break in the tension.

Mrs. Kane smiled as she approached. "Oh, you guys showed up just in time. Janice is awake, and I'm sure she'd love to see you all."

Wordlessly, we followed her to Janice's room. Stepping inside revealed a weary-worn Janice. Besides the bandage and her paler than normal skin, she looked pretty good, especially when she forced a tired grin.

"Hey, everybody," Janice said. "Glad you all could make it to my little party."

"How're you feeling, girl?" I asked when I sat by Janice on her bed. I leaned in, giving her a hug.

A nursed peeked in. "Excuse me," she said. "We have a few things we need to go through."

Mr. Kane stood. "We'll be right down the hall."

"Let us know if you guys need anything," Mrs. Kane said as they both stepped outside.

"Hey," Janice whispered, "Glad you guys got out. Did... um... "

"We did," Nate grinned as he sat on her bed. He pulled out his cellphone and began flipping through one photo after the next: ledgers, invoices, and receipts were just a few that I recognized from my vantage point.

"Can I see that?" I asked.

Nate handed it to me. I held the phone titled so Janice could get a look.

"It's okay," she said. "I'm pretty sure I won't be staring at a screen for a while. Just... um... tell me what you found."

"Yeah," I said. "Guys, let's make this quick so our girl can get her rest."

"Right," Nate said, concern in his voice. "Keep flipping until you find the documents sitting side by side."

I swiped again until I came to the image, which appeared to show two identical documents side-by-side. Then I zoomed in and saw the same date, the same account number, and the same invoice number. But they differed when they came to the bottom line: the money.

"Look at these guys," I said. "The invoice on the right has overtime on it, but the one on the left doesn't. There are also a few other line items added to the one on the right."

"I know, right?" Nate said, taking back his phone. "There's more where that came from, too." He looked directly at Marcus. "So, what're we going to do about it."

Marcus turned to me. "Do we have enough to take it to the police? If we do, what do we tell them when they ask how we got it?"

I chewed my lip for a moment as the boys looked at me. "Listen," I said. "I'm starting to think we're in way over our heads. We need to take what we have to the authorities; you know. Let them handle it."

Marcus turned to Nate.

Placing a hand to the back of his neck and rubbing it, Nate let out a sigh. "Let's get our paperwork in order," he said. "See what we have. We've got that footage of Mrs. Johnson tacking that tracking device onto Moss' car."

"That's a start," I said. "Maybe that'll pave the way for us to present our case." Though, I knew I didn't sound very confident. I wondered if the police would even take us seriously.

"Let's think about that one," Marcus said, glancing at Janice. "It's been a rough day, and one of our team members got injured. What exactly happened?"

Janice shrugged. "Created a diversion."

"You need to tell us more than that, girl," I said as I pursed my lips.

"Girl's right," Nate added. "You were supposed to pretend faint."

"Fine," Janice said with a sigh. "I didn't think fainting would be enough. So, I climbed on top of the sink and hit the sprinkler system with the end of a mop. Then I slipped."

"That was dumb," I said.

Janice laughed. "Yeah, but it sounds like it was worth it."

I nodded, though I wasn't too sure.

"Can I butt in here?" Nate asked, pointing to the spot where I sat next to Janice.

I got up, went over to Marcus, and pulled him out of the room. In the room behind us, Janice and Nate had a whispered conversation.

"Crazy day," I said to Marcus.

"I know," he said. "I think you're right. We need to rethink our approach. We can't do anything like that again."

"Do you think Moss is onto us?"

"I don't know," he said. "He seemed pretty frazzled. Like, he wasn't prepared for a flood in the bathroom."

I chuckled. "Who is?"

Marcus shrugged, about to say something when the Kanes approached with their doctor.

"Hold that thought," I said.

I peeked into the hospital room. My heart skipped a beat when I saw Nate and Janice making out.

"Hey," I said. Immediately, Nate popped upright, his face red. I continued with a laugh. "Time for Janice to get some rest. C'mon Nate."

Janice gave us a lazy wave. "See ya when I get out!"

Nate, Marcus, and I passed the Kanes and the doctor with a wave. Once in the parking lot, I couldn't help but notice a white BMW sitting, its engine running, by the curb. My eyes were drawn to Mrs. Johnson in the driver's seat. As she glared at me, I looked away.

"C'mon guys," I said under my breath. "Don't look, we're being watched."

Like the amateurs they are, Marcus and Nate both glanced at the BMW and locked eyes with Johnson. They picked up the pace, making them look even more guilty than I felt.

* * *

As I drove home, with Marcus in the front passenger seat, I kept stealing a glance in my rearview mirror. Each time, I expected to see an apparition of Johnson's BMW following us.

"That's the tenth time you've looked in the rearview mirror," Marcus said. "I really don't think she's going to follow us home."

"Maybe not," I said. "But I can't help feeling like Johnson's onto us."

"About what?" Marcus asked. "That we have a video of her with the tracking device? That we were the cause of the debacle at school?"

"She's itching to talk to me, for starters," I said. "Maybe I'm just paranoid, and she only wants to find out what I saw today."

"That's probably it," Marcus said without an ounce of conviction in his voice.

In silence, I drove the rest of the way home, making sure to keep an eye on the rearview mirror. Not that it would have done me any good. I imagined calling the police again. That same Officer Corcoran would come. She'd pull Johnson over with a report that someone suspected she was following her.

"We should find a way to trap Johnson," I said as I pulled onto our street.

"Well, we have the video," Marcus offered.

"We do." I pulled into my driveway.

"Oops," Marcus said. Wide-eyed, he looked past me.

I turned. His dad, Mr. Kahale, stormed down his porch steps.

"Marcus!" Mr. Kahale shouted. Behind him, Mrs. Kahale stood on the porch, an elbow resting on an arm crossed over her stomach. She chewed a thumbnail.

"Marcus!" Mr. Kahale shouted again. "Stop hiding in Alissa's car and get over here."

"You four," Mr. Kahale yelled again, stealing a glance at me. "You four are driving a dangerous road. You aren't the Hardy Boys. This isn't Scooby-Doo. I sure hope none of you are involved in today's incident at school."

"What's this about, Mike?" My father called from the porch of my house.

"You stay out of this, Richard!" Mr. Kahale yelled as he took long strides toward us.

My father bounded off the steps and stood between Mr. Kahale and us.

"You step out of my way," Mr. Kahale said, pushing my father.

"Mike," my father said, his voice deep and gentle. "You don't want to go down this road again."

"I —" Mr. Kahale said, confusion passing over his face. He swayed, off-balanced, then turned back inside.

About a million things passed through my mind, all of which could be summed up in the one phrase I heard Marcus utter.

"What the hell?" Marcus mumbled.

My father turned to him. "Son, are you okay?"

Marcus took a deep breath, "I... Yes."

"Has your dad been like this a lot?" My father said.

"Not since..." Marcus shook his head.

Nodding, my father said, "Okay, Marcus. You remember, you and Alissa grew up together. You're family, all of you." He gestured toward the Kahale house. "If you or your sister, or even your mother, need a place to stay for the night. You let me know."

"Thanks," Marcus said.

My father nodded. "Alissa, you and Marcus finish up here. Then come inside."

"Yes, sir," I said. When my father left, I placed a hand on Marcus' shoulder. "Are you okay?"

"I... don't know," he said, choking back tears.

Pulling him into an embrace, I rested my head upon his shoulder until I felt the gentle squeeze of his arms around my back.

As I caressed his back, I said, "Hey... um... tomorrow's Saturday. Let's go out or something. Just you and me."

He took a step back. In the twilight, his eyes twinkled. Brushing a hand against my cheek, then around my ear, he said, "So long as we don't talk about this case."

"I'm down with that," I said. "I'm also here if you want to talk about anything of this other stuff."

He offered a weak smile. "I know. Good night, Lis."

Turning, he trudged up to his house. Marcus had so much going in his life right now. More than I could even begin to imagine.

Chapter Twenty-Three

Marcus

Saturday afternoon, I stampeded down the steps, calling, "I'm headed out!"

As if she had been waiting for me, Mom stepped into the living room. "Where are you going?"

I stopped. "Lis and I are —"

"Right!" Mom interrupted me. "Take Bri with you."

I groaned. I love my sister, but I really wasn't looking to hang out with her and Alissa.

"Please, Marcus," Mom said. "Your dad will be home soon, and we both need to be alone right now."

I wanted to complain and tell her that's what Alissa and I needed. With all that had been happening, we needed time together. Time away from this case, from getting Dad cleared from an alleged theft, and from Dad's drinking. Especially Dad's drinking. Last night, he wasn't himself. Dad yelling, the way Mr. Claude talked him down. I was... stunned.

"Mom," I asked. "What's going on with you and Dad?"

In tight-lipped silence, she seemed to weigh her options. Finally, she took a breath and let it out slowly. "Marcus," she said. "Your father's a good man. This case against him doesn't seem to be settling anytime soon. We're going to see a counselor."

"Oh," I said, uncertain of what else I could say. "Um... will we be going, too?"

"Yes. But, not today. Please take your sister."

"Alright," I said.

Bri stampeded down the steps, calling, "Beat you to Lis' house!" She buzzed between us. I rolled my eyes, realizing she'd been lurking at the landing the moment I came down the steps. The door swung shut behind her.

"Thank you, Marcus," Mom said, giving me a weary smile. "This really means a lot."

For the first time, I noticed the wrinkles around her eyes and lips. Whatever they needed to discuss in counseling would be massive.

"Is there anything else you and Dad need?" I asked. "We could stay here if that would be better."

"No," she said. "There'll be plenty for you to do later. You three, just enjoy... being kids."

As I exited the house, I wondered how I could just enjoy being a kid. What Mom said seemed so weighted. I'd already asked her if they were getting a divorce. She insisted they weren't. Now, I wondered. Dad's administrative leave had already dragged on for a month. At the same time, Mr. Dunbar, his substitute, seemed to have become a permanent fixture at the school. I began to wonder whether we were even close to figuring out exactly what was going on. We had hunches, along with a rag-tag collection of documents and eye-witness accounts loosely tying everything to Moss and Johnson. But nothing that wouldn't laugh us out of a police station or a news station. Well, nothing, except for maybe the recording of Johnson tacking something to the rear of Moss' SUV. Everything at home and at school just felt wrong. Maybe Bri needed to get out just as much as I did.

* * *

"It's cool," Alissa said, giving me, then Bri, a hug when we'd trudged on over. "Bri can hang. Maybe we can go to the mall or something."

"The mall's cool," Bri said.

This night seemed like it was going to become more about Bri, than about Alissa and me. I brushed away my complaint before it could mature into resentment. Bri needed this. She needed to get away from the house.

We rode to the mall in silence. Bri had her phone out, texting, or playing a game. I occasionally glanced at Alissa. I had so much on my mind that I realized I hadn't told her how beautiful she is. Now didn't seem like the right time. Not in front of Bri.

"You wanna see a movie?" I asked.

Alissa glanced at me with a half-smile that made her dimples show. "Sure," she said, drawing the word out.

Marcus

When we pulled up, Bri unbuckled and darted out of the car so fast, I thought she had to pee. "Meeting Nyah and some other girls in the food court," she said. Before we could reply, Bri stuck out her hand, palm open, "Almost forgot."

Alissa looked at me. I looked at Bri. "Forgot what?"

"You own me ten bucks," Bri said. "Now fork it over."

I rolled my eyes, "Seriously?"

Reluctantly, I pulled out my wallet. I handed a ten to Bri, hoping I had enough to treat Alissa later.

"Thanks, big brother," Bri grinned. "You're the best! I'll meet you guys in a couple of hours, okay." She took off toward the mall entrance.

"What was that about?" Alissa asked.

"Remember that day you took her home, and Nate and I had our stakeout at school?"

Alissa laughed. "Wow! You were played."

"Yeah," I said. "Slap me in the back of the head next time I think about asking her to cover for me."

Alissa laughed as we walked toward the mall entrance. Suddenly, Alissa stopped and tugged at my hand.

I turned to her.

"How's everything at home?" Alissa asked. "I mean... Bri's been super anxious about getting out of the house."

"It's been bad," I said. "In a way, I'm glad to be out trying to solve this case for my dad. I couldn't stand just sitting around waiting for something to happen."

"I hear your dad... "Alissa's voice trailed off.

"I know," I said. "Right after Dad gets off from delivering pizzas, he's downstairs drinking. Sometimes I hear him yelling outside. Sometimes I hear him arguing with your dad, and..." I stop when I see her look away. She probably knew about this and hadn't said anything to save me the embarrassment.

"I'm sorry to hear that, Marcus," she said, stepping toward me and putting her arms around my waist. I hugged her close, feeling her warmth against my chest.

She took a step back. "I... can't imagine what you're going through. Remember, if you need to get away from all that. You can come over anytime.... um... both of you, I mean."

Her face took on a slightly rosy color as I felt my neck grow warm. We both chuckled.

"Thanks," I said as I reached out my hand. "Shall we?"

Hand in hand, we walked toward the mall. Talking to Alissa felt right. She sensed what I was going through even though I didn't give her all the details. But, in the silence, my imagination took me back to the idea of coming over to her house anytime. I had to squelch that idea right away.

I cleared my throat. "How about all those files Nate nabbed yesterday?"

Alissa gritted her teeth.

"I'm sorry," I said. "I didn't mean to."

"No, it's okay," Alissa said. "We almost can't *not* talk about it, right? But, to answer your question. I think we have enough to do something with it. Maybe draw some conclusions of our own. Because I'm pretty sure the police won't do anything with it. Maybe the news?"

"Maybe," I said. "What do you think about bringing the video Janice captured to the police. That's something, right?"

Nodding, Alissa smiled. "I think so. Johnson seems like good people, but she's definitely a little shady. Monday afternoon, we stop at the station and give it to them."

"Deal," I said, wishing I hadn't been a complete buzzkill by bringing up the topic at all. "And everything else is for another day, right?"

"Right!" Alissa perked up. "For now, it's you and me, babe. What do you want to see?"

"Something stupid-funny," I suggested.

Alissa grinned. "Not feeling like thinking right now, huh?"

"Nope," I said.

"Alright, you," she said, grabbing hold of my hand. "Let's go see what we can dig up."

There was a bounce in her step that caused me to extend my own stride as we walked. "Thanks for everything," I said.

"You bet," she said with a wink. "Besides, you're stuck with me, no matter what."

"Back atcha," I said.

She bumped her hip against mine, throwing me slightly off balance. "Maybe we should tell Bri where we're gonna be."

Suddenly, the tap of a car horn caused us both to jump and turn. We stepped to the side as a dark SUV crept toward us and stopped. While Alissa tugged at my shirt, my heart raced as the front passenger window rolled down.

"Hey," Principal Moss grinned at us. "I thought I recognized you two."

Alissa and I stared at Moss.

He chuckled. "I didn't mean to scare you or anything. Though, you two were in the middle of the roadway."

"Sorry," Alissa said. "We're glad it was you and not someone racing through the parking lot."

I added. "We'll be more careful. Um... thanks."

"Sure thing," Principal Moss said. "I hear Janice is doing better."

"She is," Alissa said. "I saw her this morning."

"You can't be too careful around those bathrooms," Principal Moss said with a wink.

"I guess, not," Alissa said, glancing at me.

"We... uh... need to get to a movie," I said.

Principal Moss nodded. "Sure, sure. You two have your fun. Monday's a big day."

As the passenger window rolled up, he maintained eye contact, grinning until he drove off.

"Freak," Alissa spat. "Was he following us?"

"If he was. That was some crazy scare tactic."

"Totally," Alissa said, taking my hand. "But let's not him ruin our day. We've got a movie to catch."

I shrugged and walked to the movie theatre with Alissa. Although Moss had been creepy in his approach, it's not like he had been stalking us. Though, I wondered if that were entirely true.

* * *

We got home late from the mall. I blamed Bri. She did not, in fact, meet up with Alissa and me when she was supposed to. We actually had to track her down. As soon as I was getting worried, she and her friends popped out of another movie theatre.

"Jeez, Bri," I shouted. "Where've you been?"

"Awww," Bri said. "Thanks for caring," She glanced at her phone just as it turned back on. "What? You sent me five texts."

I shrugged. "So... I was worried."

Her friends giggled at this. Then, one of them, Nyah, said, "We'll see you around, okay?"

I felt my face grow hot. "I *care* because of what Mom and Dad would do to me if I lost you... *again*."

"I didn't... think of that," Bri grew quiet.

"C'mon, Bri," Alissa said with laughter in her voice. "Your brother does care, and not just about getting into trouble. He loves you, even though he doesn't want to admit it."

That's not entirely true, I thought, *I had no problem admitting that I loved my sister.*

Alissa glanced behind her and flashed me a wink. Somehow, I think that comment meant more than what it seemed on the surface.

* * *

When Bri and I arrived home, my parents were sitting on the couch watching the news. Mom stood and said, "You kids want anything to eat?"

Bri darted up the steps, as I said, "No," and began to follow after her. I froze when I heard a news segment.

"More budget cuts announced today in Lenape County School District. Some are saying the cuts are related to the missing funds in the high school's athletic department."

"What!" Dad roared. He threw an empty beer can at the TV. Mom flinched when a few drops splash against her face. She wiped these off with her sleeve.

"They don't mention your name," she said. She glanced at me as she leaned in and whispered something to my dad.

Dad looked at me. "I'm sorry, son. It's just..."

"It's okay," I said. "I've got studying to do. I'll come down later."

I rounded the corner at the top of the steps and stopped where the banister meets the wall. There I heard Bri in her room, laughing loudly. I figured she was talking on the phone or texting one of her friends.

Dad cursed. "I can't believe it. I left ten-grand in the account. These lawyers and their—"

Mom shushed him, but I could still hear her. "Remember what the counselor said. The kids might be listening."

"So, what if they are?" Dad asked. He raised his voice, as if talking to me. "Maybe they need to know the truth.

I held my breath and waited. But Dad didn't say anything else. Instead, they raised the volume on the TV.

"Board meeting scheduled for the budget committee this Thursday. Those wishing to..."

I didn't wait to hear the rest. Instead, I crept into my bedroom, shut the door, and pulled my phone out of my pocket.

Group Text: *I don't know what's going on exactly. But who's in for going to budget hearing this Thursday?"*

Instantly, my phone chimed with three responses. I confirmed the time and set my phone to *do not disturb*. I needed to study, but I couldn't. I'd never been to a board meeting, but I'd heard these meetings operate as an open forum, which meant anyone was allowed to give their input. I wondered if we'd be allowed to speak. If so, maybe we could at least start to cast a shadow of suspicion on... someone. Between Moss and Johnson, I still didn't know who to believe. Plus, there was Dunbar, and I wondered if anyone else was involved.

Chapter Twenty-Four

Marcus

Before we headed to the Police Station on Sunday afternoon, we swung by Janice's house. We needed the recording of Mrs. Johnson Janice had managed to capture on her phone. I sat in the passenger seat of Alissa's Nissan, flipping over a business card from Officer Robinson.

"You really think he'll remember me?" I asked.

Alissa nodded. "Even if he doesn't, you've got the case number. Besides," — she shot me a wink and smile — "You're unforgettable."

"Right," I said, feeling heat rise to my neck. "Let's... uh... check in on Janice. Did you say she and Nate had other things to show us as well?"

Alissa, grinning ear to ear, got out of the car. I followed after her. As I stepped into the Kane's house, I was reminded of those model homes we see displayed on television ads. Clean, pristine, and painted a slate grey. Climbing the steps, I caught a whiff of something floral that seemed to cling to me, even when I reached the second floor. I followed Alissa to the third door on the right and entered Janice's room.

"Hey guys," Janice waved from where she knelt on the floor. Nate sat a few feet from her, flipping through one of several stacks of papers spread across the floor.

"You're supposed to be resting," Alissa said.

"What's all this?" I asked.

Standing, Nate said. "She *is* resting. Apparently, restrictions include no screen time. Besides, I did a lot of the close reading. Here, take a look at these." He handed me a thin stack, half of which I gave to Alissa.

"Are we still going with the discretionary-funds angle?" Alissa asked.

"I'm not sure," Nate said. "But I've got a few more theories. Shall we?"

He motioned for us to sit, which meant the floor while he took the chair. Alissa sat beside Janice while I remained standing. I didn't plan to stay for very long.

"Wait a minute," I said, flipping again through the papers he'd given me. "All of these are profit and loss reports from Booster Clubs."

"Mine too," Alissa said. "None of these are reported on the website."

"Yeah," Janice said slowly. "I know. Crazy, right?"

"Where'd you get these?" I asked. "How come you didn't show them to us the other day?"

Nate shrugged. "When I was in Moss' office, these were on his printer. I just grabbed them after seeing they were some kind of financial report."

I stared at the report for athletics. A couple fundraising activities were listed, then concession sales, donations, and income. These totaled at least ten thousand. The next section contained expenses such as merchandise, equipment, and travel.

"Okay," Alissa said. "So, what does all this mean?

Nate grinned. "Glad you asked, because I didn't know myself."

Janice chimed in. "My mom's on a booster club. She says when a club or activity needs money, they make a request to their booster, which then makes a grant to the school to make the purchase."

I felt my head spinning. Alissa looked through the papers again. "Marc, can I see yours?" She got up and stood by my side. We exchanged reports. "This all seems super complicated," she said after a moment.

"It is," Nate said. "What's worse is most parent volunteers stick to the club for a couple years, learn how to manage it, then leave it to someone else who doesn't know anything at all."

"What a minute," I said, suddenly realizing the implications of their findings. "When we broke into Moss' office, he was staring at the printer. He must've been looking for these reports. I figured he was just agitated. You know, from the diversion in the girl's bathroom."

Alissa voiced the same thing Janice and Nate were probably thinking. "Why was he printing the booster club financial reports?"

I shrugged. "We should head over to the police station. Janice, you have the video, right?"

"Here," she said. Standing, she walked over to her desk, pulled open a drawer, and handed Alissa a flash drive. "It took me forever to find one of these things, but Nate helped me transfer the mp4 from my phone to the drive."

"Thanks, guys," I said, looking at my friends. "For everything."

"No doubt, bro," Nate said. "Hey! Janice and I were talking. Maybe I should come with you. You know, since I was there with you."

Alissa and I exchanged a look. "That's cool," Alissa said. "You're right. Officer Robinson might wonder why you didn't show up. That, and," — she gave me a nudge — "Marcus here was worried your guy wouldn't remember him."

I rolled my eyes. "Thanks, Lis."

Nate and Janice laughed. "Anyway," Janice said. "While you guys are out, Lis and I can look into what Moss was doing with those reports."

"Definitely," Alissa and I said simultaneously. We laughed, while Nate and Janice seemed to share a knowing look.

As we headed out the door, I wondered if those reports were on Moss' printer for a reason. If so, did that reason have something to do with Mom and Dad?

* * *

I stood, paced, checked my phone, then paced again.

"Seriously, bro," Nate said as he stretched, allowing himself to take up even more of the chair he sat in. "Sit down. You're making the desk sergeant nervous."

I glanced at the desk sergeant, an older woman, who shot me an emotionless nod. I plopped myself in the seat beside Nate.

"I'm sorry," I said. "I'm just nervous. What if Officer Robinson doesn't come? What if he's late? What if he calls our parents? That'll blow the whole thing."

Suddenly, Nate shot out of his seat. Smiling with confidence, he directed his attention toward the officer walking our way. When the officer waved at us, I stood and attempted to match Nate's composure.

"Nathan Wilson," Officer Robinson announced while he extended his hand. Nate took it, and the two shared a firm, friendly handshake.

"Good to see you again, sir," Nate said. "You remember Marcus Kahale."

"Of course," Officer Robinson said as he shook my hand. "Nice to see you both again."

"Likewise," I said.

Officer Robinson kept his gaze on me. "What can I do for you?"

I cleared my throat. "A month ago, you were at the scene of a hit and run..." Seeing Officer Robinson nod, I continued. "You took our eyewitness statements."

"Yes," Officer Robinson said with a chuckle. "Mr. Wilson's testimony was unorthodox."

"That's me," Nate said, salting his voice with a hint of sarcasm. "Unorthodox."

With a thin smile, Officer Robinson said, "Well, that's..."

As his voice trailed off, I suddenly felt the weight of the flash drive in my pocket. "We have something for you."

As I fished the flash drive out, Nate spoke. "A friend of ours captured something on video that might help in the investigation."

I handed the flash drive to Officer Robinson, who took it with narrowed eyes. "You want to keep this friend anonymous," he said. "So, what's on the drive?" He pulled out a notepad.

Nate spoke. "Mrs. Annette Johnson, one of our school administrators. She seems to be sticking something on the back of Mr. Wayne Moss' car."

Officer Robinson paused in his notetaking to peer at us. He let out a sigh. "And you think she was the one who placed the device we found on Mr. Moss' SUV?"

Feeling a little more confident, I said, "We don't think, sir. We know."

Cracking a smile, Officer Robinson said, "Looks like we've got a couple of junior detectives on our hands." He paused. "How long have you had this?"

After exchanging a look and a nod, Nate and I spoke at the same time.

"Not long," he said.

"Since the day after," I said.

Laughing, Officer Robinson said, "Which is it?"

With a tilt of his head toward me, Nate said, "What he said."

Sighing, Officer Robinson said, "Why were you holding this for so long?"

"Go ahead," Nate said. "You tell him."

I blurted out the first thing that came to my mind that didn't sound like a lie. "We didn't want to get our assistant principal in trouble by making a false accusation." I took a breath, then added, "So, we had to be sure. And now we are."

Officer Robinson seemed to stand there, as though testing my statement's weight. He stuffed the flash drive into his pocket. "There's nothing else?" He asked.

"No, sir," I said, feeling like I should share more even though I knew what we had would sound completely ridiculous. Not to mention, irrelevant to his investigation.

Nate stuck out his hand, "Thank you for your time, Officer Robinson. Hopefully, that video will help."

"Maybe," Officer Robinson said, shaking Nate's hand, then my own. His gaze seemed to linger on me for a moment after he released his grip. "You boys, let me know when you have more to share."

Though my ears seemed to burn, I forced a smile. "We will. Take care."

Once in the safety of Nate's Jeep, Nate turned to me. "Bro, you really need to work on reading my signals."

"Me?" I said. "What about you? What part of a nod is supposed to communicate *Not long*?"

"What?" Nate shook his head. "No. You were telling me to go ahead and speak."

I huffed. "Sounds like we were both a little off, yeah?"

Nate laughed. "Yeah."

He raised a fist. I returned the gesture with a quick bump.

"Let's get out of here," I said. "Maybe the girls managed to find out something about why

Moss might've had those reports from the booster clubs."

Grinning, Nate pulled out of the parking lot. "No doubt. They're definitely more in sync than we were today."

Chapter Twenty-Five

Alissa

Monday morning seemed to drone on endlessly as our A. P. U.S. History teacher discussed what I assumed to be some terrible moment in the colonial period. With Janice still recovering from what thankfully turned out to be only a mild concussion, the class was far less interesting than it normally would be.

The intercom buzzed. "Please send Alissa Claude to the office."

Dread seemed to drop to my stomach as I stood. *The incident* happened on Friday. Since then, Johnson had waited for us, glared at us, in the parking lot outside of the hospital. Then, Moss pulled up to Marcus and me in the parking lot at the mall. His not so coded message stuck with me, *You two have your fun. Monday's a big day.* So, a call to the office wasn't a shocker.

When I got there, Marcus and Nate were already waiting outside. While Nate sat there, his leg shaking nervously, Marcus paced. As he turned, his eyes met my own and brightened.

Marcus forced a grin. "Glad you could make it to the party."

"I guess you know what this is about," I said, looking from Marcus to Nate.

"Yup!" Nate said. He lowered his voice, "Don't worry, though. Camera's were disabled."

Principal Moss' door opened. He glanced at us, then down the hallway, as if expecting someone else. "Well, come on in."

The three of us shrugged. Principal Moss muttered something about staff attendance then motioned for us to come in. Taking a few cautious steps inside, I half expected Johnson standing in the corner, smirking at me. She wasn't there. Behind us, the door clicked shut. I decided I wouldn't ask if Mrs. Johnson would be joining us. Though, as we all took a seat, I wondered if she'd been arrested

"It's funny," Moss said, as he took a seat. "On Friday, Janice was in the bathroom when the pipes spontaneously burst. Alissa, you were hanging out by the bathroom, where your best friend happened to be knocked out. And Marcus, you were at my office. For what, I'm not sure. But I know it wasn't to ask me about the field trips."

Marcus looked down, guilt radiating from his face. I nudged him, trying to be all discreet. I wasn't.

"So, Alissa," Moss said. "You have something to say?"

"I'm pretty sure our parents should be with us," I said.

Moss' chair creaked as he leaned back, crossing his hands behind his head. "Okay."

I waited. "Okay?' I asked. As Principal Moss and I measured each other, I began to realize I held the gaze of a man whose dealings were, at the very least, shady. No way he should have access to the booster club funds. According to Janice's mom, they're running as 501c3's to protect against fraud.

Nate and Marcus shifted beside me.

I began to rise. "Let's go then."

"Just a moment," replied Moss. He walked over to his drawer as I plopped back in the seat. "Here's what I don't understand." He rifled through the contents of his drawer. "I'm missing a few files."

"Principal Moss," I said. "You gave us some documents from that cabinet weeks ago."

"I did," Moss said. It wasn't a question. "Yes, but somehow other related files went missing, as well."

Nate cleared her throat. "Maybe... Maybe they were stuck to the files you gave them. You know, static electricity."

Moss scanned my face, then his roving eyes locked onto Marcus. "And what do you think, Mr. Kahale!" He seemed to intentionally emphasize Marcus' last name, as though he had a personal vendetta against his father.

"To be honest, sir," Marcus began. "I wouldn't know what you intended to give Alissa and Janice. Alissa showed me the files. I had no idea what I was looking at."

Moss and Marcus seemed to be measuring each other with their gaze.

"Fine," Moss said. "I'll bite... for now... Nate, perhaps you'll be able to clear this little mystery up. You're good with stuff like that, right?"

"If you mean financials," Nate said. "Nope. No good at stuff like that."

With a narrow-eyed gaze, Moss shifted from Nate to Marcus, then to me.

"If there's nothing else," I said. "I really have to get back to A.P. U.S. History. Big test, you know." I forced a laugh. "Want to keep my GPA up."

Moss sighed. "I'll write you all a pass. But I'm keeping my eye on you three. None of you are cleared from last week's little fiasco with the water. As soon as we're able to recover the video footage..." His voice trailed off as he scribbled on three different forms. He handed one to each of us.

"Don't you mean the four of us," Marcus offered. "Don't forget about Janice."

Moss chucked. "Of course. Four. You should expect the next summons to my office to include a conference with each of your parents."

The three of us exited the office. When we were a safe distance away from the office, I breathed a little easier. We all did.

"He's on to us," I said.

"Clearly," Marcus and Nate said together.

"So, what now," I asked. "Did you notice Moss seemed to be looking for someone else?"

"I did," Marcus said. "I don't think she's in the building."

My breath caught in my throat. "Arrested?"

"No way," Nate said. "Too soon. We've got to figure something out. Maybe trail her."

"You've got to be kidding—"

"Aren't you three supposed to be in class?" asked Dunbar as he raised his voice.

The three of us spun, spotting Dunbar coming toward us.

"We were just headed to class," I said, handing Dunbar the pass when he was close enough.

Dunbar took it, gave it a quick narrowed-eyed glance, then handed it back to me. "What did you three do?"

"If you don't mind," Marcus said. "We really do need to get to class."

"You're right," Dunbar said. "And I've been told to keep my eye out. Ms. Claude, head to class. Marcus and Nate, I'll escort you two."

I turned away.

I trusted Marcus wholeheartedly. He and Nate would figure something out, though I hoped it wouldn't be something that would cause any more of us to get injured. Judging from Moss' behavior, I had a feeling we were getting close to the truth and he had no idea how to handle us. We already shook the nest. Now, we needed a way to figure out how to catch those involved in this scandal that had put Mr. Kahale out of work and our season on an indefinite hold. All the paperwork we'd acquired held the key, but we were missing something. We had our hunches, but I wondered if we had enough to catch the attention of a news station. We'd already attempted to go to the police once. The officer took the video and said he would check in on the evidence. Mrs. Johnson wasn't in school today, but that didn't mean she'd been arrested.

As I rounded the end of the hallway, I thought I heard Marcus say something strange.

Chapter Twenty-Six

Marcus

"I'm sorry, but what exactly are you suggesting?' I said, loud enough for Alissa to hear. Dunbar walked beside Nate and me until Alissa was out of earshot.

Stopping to look at me, Dunbar said, "You know, that ticket booth held some serious cash."

My eyes followed Dunbar when he looked to his left. Alissa scurried around the corner and out of sight. He looked back at Nate and me. Then, the corners of his mouth curled slowly as he leaned toward us like we were sharing a secret. "You know," Dunbar whispered. "A couple of kids could do quite a bit with the kind of cash your pop kept in that old shed."

"Okay," I said. I couldn't tell whether Dunbar was baiting me or giving me the skinny on what was really going on at this school.

He nodded his head slowly and winked at me. "Untraceable cash. If you know what I mean."

"We don't," Nate said. "And you need to back up. If you haven't noticed, you're on camera." Nate pointed at the ceiling.

Dunbar took a quick glance, then grinned. "Don't worry about that. Here, let's try a different approach." His face scrunched up, like he was in pain. Then it softened as a smile formed on his face. "Why do you think we aren't getting new uniforms or those away games? Imagine if someone just returned what wasn't his. You might get what you want."

"Sure," I said. "That'll be great... if that happens, I mean."

"Good," Dunbar said, clapping me on the shoulder. "Let's get you two to class."

As I followed a few paces behind Dunbar, I hoped my response didn't give the impression that Nate and I had stolen these supposed funds out of the shed.

Dunbar spoke again, though he didn't turn, or wait for us to fall in step beside him. "You know, the sports and drama programs will most certainly be cut if we can't get the finances in order."

"Makes sense," I said. "Why are you telling us this?"

He stopped. "Don't you know? I'm in charge of athletics now. Your father isn't coming back."

Heat rose to my neck, then to my face, as I stared at Dunbar.

"Why look so surprised?" He asked. "Surely, your father told you this."

My throat tightened, and my voice cracked when I spoke. "Yeah. I'm... just surprised, you know, because you're telling me this."

Dunbar nodded. "Don't worry, though. I won't hold anything your father did against you." He took a step toward me. "Unless I need to. Do I need to?"

"No, sir," I said. "You don't. Can we get to class now?"

Marcus

With a sweeping arc of his arm, he gestured toward the open hallway, leaving us to walk freely toward our classroom. As we did, my mind swirled.

"Dude," Nate said under his breath when we were out of earshot. "Don't let that blowhard get to you. He doesn't know anything."

"There's no way you can know that," I said.

Shrugging, Nate said. "Suit yourself. Then, let's stick to what we do know."

"Johnson," I said. "Don't worry, I'll think of something."

We fist-bumped and parted ways to our separate classes. Entering the classroom and taking a seat, I stared at a barrage of equations scribbled all across the whiteboard. Though I missed a lot of instruction, I didn't bother to catch up. Instead, a plan started forming in my mind.

I slipped out my phone.

Group Text: *Guys. Meet after practice. We've gotta track you-know-who.*

Alissa: *Better not be dangerous.*

When I was about to reply, I suddenly felt a presence by my side. A few sniggers rippled across the room. I looked up.

My teacher held his hand out, palm open. "You can put that away, or you can give it to me."

"Sorry," I said, turning my cell phone off and stuffing it back into my pocket.

When my teacher walked away and recommended with the instruction no one was listening to, I imagined my plan playing out. Though I knew it wasn't dangerous, I wondered if what I intended was even legal.

* * *

After practice, we met in the parking lot. The rest of the day had been nothing more than ordinary, except for catching Alissa in the hallway and letting her know of our... I mean, my plans for after school. She had rolled her eyes with skepticism but told me she'd check on the legality of what I intended.

"So," Alissa said, dropping her gear off in her car. "I did some research. We should definitely avoid recording someone against their consent."

"Huh," Nate said. "If the police even looked at the video, there's no way they'd be able to use it to press any charged. Fingerprints will have to do that."

"Fair enough," I said. "Who's hungry? We can hash out the details over pizza.'

"Should we ride over, or walk?" Alissa asked.

"Walk," Nate said. Without waiting for a response, he headed toward the street. "I've been sitting all day."

Just before the crosswalk, Nate pounded the push-to-walk button. He turned to us, grinning. "If you two get any closer, I'm going to throw-up."

"You're one to talk," Alissa said.

With a ding, the signal switched to walk.

"So, not cool," Nate said as he stepped into the street.

I felt my own face flush and reminded myself to avoid anything more than holding hands with Alissa in public. Suddenly, I heard the rattle of an old engine. Where, moments before, the street was empty, a pale blue car sped up as though aiming for us. Grabbing Nate in the same instant, I pulled him back to the curb. In a blur of blue, the car, an old sedan, maybe a Honda, sped by, feet away from us, horn blaring.

"Whoah!" I exclaimed. "We need to keep our heads up."

"Yeah," Nate said, breathing heavily and clinging to me. "Thanks."

"You okay?" Alissa asked as Nate released his grip on me. "Maybe we should just go back and drive over."

"I think we're good," I said. When no one answered, I added with very little confidence, "Right?"

"I'm good," Nate said, hitting the button one more time. "Like you said. We need to keep our heads up."

We waited, carefully monitoring the road as cars flew by. When the light changed, we looked both ways five times before running across the street. Once on the other side, Nate turned to us.

"We must be getting close!" He exclaimed.

I wondered if he referred to his near-death experience. "How so?" I asked.

"That car," he said. "Did you recognize it?" His eyes, full and piercing, seemed to measure each of us in turn.

"I didn't —" Alissa began.

"Holy crap!" I interrupted her.

"Yes!" Nate clapped his hand once and pointed at me. "I'm not one hundred percent on this, but it looks like that car that ran Moss off the road. Did you get a license? "

I shook my head.

"No matter," Nate said, pulling out his phone. "We can call Officer Robinson and give him an approximate time."

"While you do that," Alissa said. "Marcus and I will go inside and order."

Nate, phone already to his ear, shot us a thumbs up.

As Alissa and I took a seat, I said. "Listen to this..." I told her about our encounter with Dunbar after our little meeting with Moss."

Alissa said, "I wondered what was going on with you and Dunbar. I can't believe you didn't tell me about it earlier."

"Sorry," I said. "I kind of passed it off as Dunbar being... I don't know... Dunbar?"

"Bro," Nate laughed as he entered. "It sounded like he was baiting us. Which means he's either involved or a dumb lackey who doesn't know what's really going on."

"Maybe," I said. "But I wouldn't call Dunbar dumb."

For a minute, no one spoke as we all seemed to muse things over.

Alissa sighed. "Well, whatever the case may be. We're definitely on Moss' radar."

"Agreed," Nate said. He looked at me and grinned. "Alright, *M.*, what's the plan?"

My mind seemed to draw a blank. Earlier today, I imagined us following Johnson all over the place, then easily catching her in some crime. Now, I wasn't so sure.

Alissa clearly noticed. "Tell ya what, Marc. I'll order while you think it over."

Laughing, I said. "Give me a minute. I'm going to check in with my dad to do a little fact-checking of Dunbar's claims about the money being in the ticket-booth. Maybe tonight. My mom and Bri are at some middle school function."

Nate added. "Don't forget about Dunbar's claims that your dad isn't coming back to school."

I nodded. "I'm not sure if that's a good idea yet. It could backfire, you know."

Alissa stood with a smile. "You know what? I'm going to order a cheese pizza. That okay?" Without waiting for us to answer, she waltzed on over to the counter.

"She's got a point," Nate said. "There's not much we can do about it right now. Let's eat, relax, and lay low for a while."

"Good idea," I said. "We'll make ourselves scarce while we figure out what we're going to do about all the evidence we've gathered. We'll need a solid presentation if we even get a chance to speak at the hearing."

With that, Alissa returned. "Pizza's ordered. No more talk on this right now, okay?"

We nodded in agreement, though Nate and I locked eyes. He flashed me a sly grin. I didn't expect him to be inactive, but I knew he'd lay low.

Marcus

When the pizza arrived, still steaming, everyone grabbed a slice. As for me, I chewed on the idea of approaching Dad with Dunbar's allegations. Then, I realized, Nate never did tell me how to deal with a drunk dad. So, I hoped Dad would be sober and lucid when I found the best time to talk to him.

* * *

"Dad," I called when I entered the house.

It was a little after 8 pm. "Dad," I called again. When I closed the door, I kicked something that was sent down the hallway with a hollow, metallic rattle. I picked it up and found myself holding an empty beer can.

With my bag strapped to my back and the beer can in my hand, I entered the living room. There, Dad slouched on the couch and snored loudly with his head bobbing gently against his chest. There was a pile of empties on the coffee table and one in his hand, resting precariously on his knee.

I plopped myself on the couch. As my weight shifted on the cushion, Dad popped awake with a quick snore.

"Huh?" He said and looked at me. His eyes were puffy and bloodshot.

Thankfully Mom and Bri would be out for a while. Though, I wondered whether Dad had started drinking before or after they left.

"I'm home," I offered.

"You're home," he repeated. "You're too young to drink."

I placed the empty can on the coffee table and said, "It's yours. I found it in the foyer."

"Oh," Dad said. "When did you get home?"

"A few minutes ago," I said.

He shifted in his seat and leaned toward me, squishing his eyebrows together. "Did you eat?" Dad asked.

I held my breath when I caught a whiff of sour beer on his breath. I'd never seen him like this before. It was embarrassing.

"I just came home to clean up," I answered. "Then, I'm going to study at Alissa's house."

"Sweet kid," my dad mused. "You two are right for each other."

"Thanks," I said. This was getting super uncomfortable. "Have Mom and Bri been home yet?"

Dad shook his head. "They'll be home around nine. Looks like it's just you and me tonight." He seemed to perk up, "You hungry?"

"We ate after practice," I said, noticing his shoulders slump and his face take on a faraway gaze as though I'd disappointed him.

"Dad," I continued. "You remember when I told you about the ticket booth being broken into, right?'

"Yup," he said, then he spoke in barely a whisper. "Real shame."

"You were pretty freaked out about it like there was more than just some papers," I said.

"Who told you?" Dad said, turning toward me suddenly.

"You did," I said, feeling the intensity of Dad's gaze on me. "So did Dunbar."

Dad stood, though wobbly, and reached for his phone. "I'm going to call that man right now. What business does he have...?"

His voice trailed off as he focused on dialing the phone. I reached for the phone, and, somehow, he let me slide it with ease from his grasp. Plopping himself down, Dad said, "The money's gone."

"How much is missing?" I asked.

"Forty-six hundred," Dad mumbled as he placed his face into his hands. He wept. "It was our biggest game, yet. Now, it's gone."

I wanted to ask him why he'd leave that amount of money in a dilapidated shed, even if it was locked up. Instead, I asked, "Are you coming back to work?"

Looking up, he turned to me. Tears streaked his face. He didn't wear that look well.

Shrugging, Dad said, "I really don't know. Lawyers can't find the paperwork. I've got no record of past deposits. I'm... I'm done for." When he placed his hand on my knee, I flinched. "I'm sorry, son. I've... I've let you down."

I stood. "Dad, you didn't let me down."

Dad sniffled. "Thanks, son. You're a good kid, despite what Moss has told me."

My eyes grew wide. "What did you say?"

He waved a hand. "Something about you helping Nate steal some paperwork out of his office. He couldn't prove it. If he could, you'd be suspended."

"Right," I said. "So, I'm going to go upstairs, clean-up, then head on over to Alissa's house."

"You have fun," Dad said, seeming to sink deeper into the sofa.

I ran upstairs, trying to process everything that had just happened. While warm water washed the sweat of a great run off my body, it didn't help to bring any clarity to the jarring image of Dad slouched and snoring drunkenly on the couch. Nor did it help to clear my head about an impending suspension for my friends and me. But, if the risk we took to make Dad's name paid off, I'd take a suspension. Maybe Alissa would, too. I wasn't sure about Janice and Nate. They'd need something bigger, like a full-blown FBI investigation. Well... maybe that was too big of an ask.

In less than five minutes, I was bounding down the steps. "Bye, Dad," I said, and was out the door before he could respond. In another fifteen steps, I was at Alissa's door.

Before I could even knock, Mr. Claude opened the door. His figure, always imposing, seemed to frame the entire doorway as though he'd grown since last I'd seen him. Or, maybe it was the silence that felt imposing. Whatever it was, I felt like he was sizing me up. I jumped when he cleared his throat. When he finally did speak, it was clear that he made an attempt to soften the gruffness of his voice.

"I'm sorry, Marcus," he said. "Alissa's been suspended. It's my understanding you have, too."

I didn't respond because the way Dad said it, it sounded like *maybe*. Then again, Dad probably didn't catch everything Moss told him over the phone. I trusted Mr. Claude did

"Does your father know you're over here?" Mr. Claude asked.

"I'm not sure," I said. "He's... Ummm... "

Mr. Claude nodded. "Drunk?" He asked, then paused as he seemed to read my expression. "Your mom told me before she and Bri went out."

"Oh," I said. "But they'll be back soon." Even as I spoke, I knew my own voice betrayed the frail hope I clung to.

Mr. Claude seemed to sense it, too. A look, like steel, seemed to pass over his face. "Come inside," he said.

He stepped to the side to allow room for me to enter. Once in the foyer, the door behind me closed with a gentle click. Mr. Claude held me in his gaze for a moment before he offered me a warm, sad smile.

"There's a lot we need to talk about," he said. Without another word, he walked toward the living room. I followed him, knowing full well he expected me to do so.

Chapter Twenty-Seven

Alissa

"There's a lot we need to talk about," I heard my father say softly to Marcus.

I stood at the top of steps, just out of sight of the door, even though my father had explicitly said, "You best be in your room when he comes in the door."

I was ready to dip, thinking that was the end of it when I heard my father ask, "Does your father know you're over here?" With that comment, I knew my father was about to send Marcus packing for the night. But, then, the word *drunk* and the definitive way my father told Marcus, without actually telling Marcus, that his mom and Bri weren't coming home tonight.

Sensing what was left of Marcus' own feeble optimism drain right out of him, my heart broke. I couldn't imagine how bad things were for his mom to check out with Bri without telling him. If my mother did that, it would tear me apart. I felt that now for Marcus. Placing a knuckle between my teeth, I bit back my onslaught of tears.

"Follow me," my father said.

"Okay," Marcus mumbled.

As their footsteps faded into the living room, I sat on the top step, causing the floors to creak like thunder throughout our rickety old house.

My father greeted the momentary silence with his own heavy footsteps that brought him to the bottom of the steps. He crossed his arms, seeming to dare me to offer an excuse for disappointing him one more time.

"Alissa Imani Claude," he said, letting my name reach my ears with a hiss like he was afraid Marcus would hear him. "What did I tell you?"

"Sorry," I managed to squeak.

My father shook his head before he turned and directed his next remark to Marcus, who was still out of sight. "I wanted this little conversation to be private," he said. Letting out a sigh, he continued, "But, I suspect you'd tell Alissa everything, anyway."

Marcus' muffled voice answered him. "She can join us. I mean... if you don't mind."

My father, ever the expert at expressions, shot me dagger eyes as he hissed, "Don't you think you're off the hook, young lady. C'mon now."

Slowly, I stood as I kept my head down. As I descended the steps and passed my father, I hoped my posture would communicate some semblance of remorse. Though, I wasn't sure if I felt worse about being caught or worse about disobeying my father. To be honest, twenty minutes ago, I thought l couldn't've felt any worse about being suspended, then grounded. But, now, I'd take that feeling back in a heartbeat.

I followed my father into the living room until he took a seat in one of the wingback chairs.

"Alissa," my father said, gesturing to a seat on the other side of the sofa.

Sighing, I obeyed, though I allowed myself a quick peek at Marcus. When he returned my gaze, I offered him a weak smile, something I hoped would let him know I still had his back. I caught a slight smile from Marcus, though his look of bewilderment returned almost as quickly.

Sitting in the wing chair, my father made an attempt to compose himself. Lips pressed together and eyes closed, he breathed through his nose. With a raised eyebrow, Marcus glanced at me. I knew better to say anything. I shook my head.

"Marcus," my father said with a sad smile. "There are things you need to know about your father."

The sofa creaked as Marcus, mouth clammed shut and eyes wide, slid forward.

Chapter Twenty-Eight

Marcus

My head spun as I kept my eyes fixed on Mr. Claude. Clearing his throat, he looked at the floor. I imagined he'd tell me Dad was somehow involved in this alleged money scandal. To my right, Alissa shifted closer to me. I appreciated her support, though I wondered if she already knew.

Mr. Claude cleared his throat. "To clear the air," he said. "I don't believe your dad has stolen any money."

I let out a breath I didn't realize I'd been holding. Alissa did the same, though vocalizing it with a squeak.

"Now," Mr. Claude said. "Don't get ahead of yourselves. Marcus, this is important, so you need to listen carefully. Okay?"

I nodded. "Yes, sir."

"You're sure you want Alissa to hear this?"

"Please," I said, glancing at Alissa. With a reassuring smile, she nodded.

"Alright, then," Mr. Claude said. "Alissa, you make sure you don't go telling anyone else about this."

"I won't," Alissa said in a hoarse whisper.

This seemed to satisfy her father. Mr. Claude continued. "Marcus, long before you were born, I sponsored your father in A. A. This past month, I tried to keep it on the down-low. Your father assured me it was only a few drinks. But, since our weekend at the beach, it's only gotten worse. With the drinking, then the yelling, then the verbal abuse —"

Someone in the room let out a gasp and a whimper. When Alissa took my hand, I realized it was I who had made that sound.

"Listen," Mr. Claude said. "You can stay here, in the guest room, of course. Or I can take you to stay with your mom and Bri at your grandparents' house for the week."

Between the three of us, the silence seemed to last forever. I felt betrayed, like everyone else around me knew Dad had been harboring a demon. In a desperate need for answers, I wanted to scream, *Somebody, say something!*

Beside me, Alissa chewed her lower lip. I realized, like me, she was hearing this news for the first time. I also knew I needed to be with Mom and Bri. Still, I needed to stay around here. Dad needed me, and I needed to be here for Alissa. We needed to stick to our plan to make an appearance at the budget hearing.

"Tell you what," Mr. Claude said. "I know you've got a lot on your plate. I also know why you did what you did to get yourself suspended."

He chuckled. Realizing my mouth had fallen open, I clammed it shut.

"Let's just say," Mr. Claude said. "You and Nate did a good thing going to Officer Robinson with the evidence you had."

Mentally, I kicked myself as I realized we could've gone to Mr. Claude this whole time. As a self-defense trainer for the police, he could've gotten us connected a lot sooner.

Standing, Mr. Claude said, "Marcus, I'm going to go check on your father. I'll let him know you're over here. With some luck, he'll be ready to talk."

Nodding in agreement, I said, "Should I come with you?"

He seemed to ponder that question for a moment. Directing his next remark to Alissa, he said, "Why don't you two stay over here. I believe you've got a lot of planning to do if you're going to make the right impression at the budget hearing." He directed his gaze toward me. "Are you feeling up to it?"

Leaning toward me, Alissa whispered in my ear with a hint of laughter in her voice, "Your mouth is open again."

"There's... I don't know... a lot," I said, helpless to form a coherent thought.

"Take it easy, then," Mr. Claude said. "I'm going to pay your father a visit. You should call your mother. If you decide to follow your plans to go before the board, you let me know. I can sit with you. Okay?"

I managed a nod. When Mr. Claude left the room, Alissa's hand, soft and warm, took my own, giving it a gentle squeeze. Then, there on the couch, with my best friend by my side, I cried. For what Mom must've been going through. For Bri, who probably glued herself to her phone as an escape from something she'd managed to intuit long before I had. For Dad, for a reputation now ruined, but in whose eyes?

Doubt about Dad, like a shadow in my periphery, had been creeping over me throughout our investigation. Now, I could no longer recognize him through this shroud of skepticism. Eight words fought their way to the forefront of my mind: *He's not the man you thought he was.*

* * *

Alissa and I still sat on the living room couch when Mrs. Claude finally came through the front door. I stood when Mrs. Claude came over to me, arms open wide.

"Marcus, honey, I'm so sorry about everything that's happening." Stepping back, she gave me a weary but warm smile. "Your mom and sister are settled in. When you're ready, give them a call. Your mom really wants to talk to you."

"I will," I said, though I wasn't sure when I'd be ready to call Mom. I wondered what she could possibly add that Mr. Claude hadn't already told me.

"Okay," Mrs. Claude said. She directed her next comment to Alissa. "Is your father back?"

When Alissa answered in the negative, Mrs. Claude responded with a sigh. "I'll be upstairs. You kids holler on up if you need anything."

"Thanks, mom," Alissa said. She turned to me. "Do you want to call your mom?"

I shook my head.

Alissa took a deep breath. "What do you want to do?"

Finally, I shook my head. "I'm feeling useless right now. Do you think we could look through that paperwork?"

"Are you sure?" Alissa asked, her brows furrowed.

"Maybe," I said. "I don't know."

"Just in case," Alissa said. "I'll be right back."

As she darted up the steps, I couldn't help but grin. In a few minutes, she came back down, box in hand. Then, she placed the box in the middle of the floor and sat cross-legged in from of it.

"What?" Alissa said with a hint of laughter in her voice. "You're staring."

"Mind if I join you?" I asked, trying to be playful, to take my mind off things.

"Sure," Alissa said.

When I shifted to the floor, she handed me a manila folder. Thumbing through one page, then the next, my mind kept going back to images of Dad. Him, several months earlier, being confronted by an upset Moss. Then, the sudden binge drinking on top of his attempts to look presentable in a pizza uniform.

"You aren't seeing this, are you?" Alissa asked.

My fingers clutched a half-turned paper. I shifted my attention to Alissa. Her eyes, a dark caramel, glistened with what I sensed to be concern. Waiting me out in silence, she bit her lower lip.

"Not really," I said at last. "How about you?"

She shook her head. "It's going on eleven. You really should call your mom."

Letting out a yawn, I said, "I guess."

"Should I leave you alone? Or..."

"Stay," I said, glad she offered. Though, I knew she would've stayed, even insisted upon it. I would've let her, too.

Turning my phone on caused several *dings* as messages and voicemail notifications popped up. Mom had left several voicemails, none of which I bothered to listen to. Likewise, I thumbed through and didn't answer several text messages from Bri and Nate. I'd get back to Bri tomorrow. Nate, on the other hand,

I wasn't so sure about. He probably had some more wacky ideas he wanted to pitch to Alissa and me. I decided I'd veto his ideas before they had a chance to take root.

When I dialed Mom's number, it rang several times before she finally picked up.

"Oh, sweetie," she said. "I'm so glad you called. How are things?"

"Fine, I guess," I said. However, I resented that Mom managed to capture the entirety of tonight's revelations with *things*. "I'm at Alissa's house. I'm... going to stay here for a few days?" I asked this as a question, not a statement.

"That's okay," Mom said. "Richard called. He said he'd fill you in on —"

"But why'd you leave?" I asked. "You didn't even call or tell me."

"I'm sorry," she said with tears in her voice. "I called. Bri texted you. You didn't answer. I had to get your sister out of there."

Feeling about an inch tall, I managed to squeak out. "Oh... what happened?"

"Your father. He's not in a good place right now," she said. "I couldn't let your sister see him like that. I'm sorry you had to see him like that."

I felt my throat tighten as heat rose to my eyes. I sniffed. "Did you leave him... I mean... for good?"

"Nothing like that," she said. "We need to have some space until..."

Her voice trailed off, replaced by tears. "I'm so sorry. I should've seen this coming. Should've acted sooner."

"Well," I said, trying to figure out how to end this call. I glanced at Alissa for support.

Scooting closer to me, she placed her hand on my back. Somehow, her warmth brought my comfort. "You're doing great," Alissa said.

I nodded.

"Is Alissa with you?" Mom asked as if she could see right through the phone.

"Yes," I said.

"Can I talk to her?"

Taking the phone from me, Alissa placed it to her ear. She listened intently, nodding to whatever mom was saying. Occasionally, Alissa responded with phrases like "Yes, ma'am" or "I will" until she finally said, "He's in good hands." She handed the phone back to me.

"Hey," I said when I placed the phone back up to my ear.

"Marcus," Mom said. "I hear you've got some plans for clearing your father."

"Yeah," I said, wondering how much Mr. Claude found out from Alissa and how much he figured out on his own.

"Mind her parents, Mr. and Mrs. Claude," Mom said. "Can you do that for me?"

"I will," I said.

"I love you, sweety," Mom said. "We'll see you in a couple of days."

"I... love you, too, Mom."

With that, I hung up the phone suddenly aware of the exchange of heat between Alissa and me. Sitting side by side, listening to each other breath, slowly, steadily, we lost ourselves in each other's' eyes.

Suddenly I sensed the weight of the room shift. Almost in the same instant, a voice cleared. Alissa and I scooted away from each other and looked up.

"Well," Mr. Claude said. "Marcus, why don't you get settled in the guest room." He held out an old duffel bag I recognized as my own.

For a moment, Alissa and I fumbled with the paperwork we barely got a chance to look at.

"Don't worry about that," Mrs. Claude said. "You two can get to that in the morning before I come back with the schoolwork you'll be missing."

Rising to our feet, I said, "Um... goodnight, Lis."

"Goodnight, Marcus," Alissa said.

Alissa turned to the steps leading up to her bedroom, while I turned toward the archway where her parents stood. Beyond that, lay the guest room.

"One more thing, you two," Mr. Claude said. He held out his hand into which we both surrendered our cell phones. "Can't have you two texting each other all night," he said. "Punishment, aside. You two will need to be extra fresh in the morning if you're going to get a jump on all the work you've got ahead of you."

Sleep, I hoped, would give me a fresh perspective, but I also had my doubts. I wanted to believe Dad was innocent, but I realized now his behavior, despite what Mr. Claude said, made him look totally guilty. I also wanted to know what happened next door when Mr. Claude got my bag. He must've talked to Dad. Despite my feelings of betrayal, I also worried about him. Then, my mind shifted. As much as I liked my friends, I hoped Janice and Nate weren't coming over tomorrow. I wasn't sure I wanted them around right now, not that I was mad at them. No, I needed my head on straight, without any wild ideas that would amount to breaking school rules anymore. Or, worse, breaking the law. I had a feeling it would be Alissa and me putting the finishing touches on this case with Mr. Claude there to guide us. I knew that would be for the best. I only hoped it would be enough.

Chapter Twenty-Nine

Alissa

We, joined by Nate and Janice, stood outside of the school district offices. Though Janice seemed to have mostly recovered from the concussion, she still clung to Nate like a lifeline. Or, maybe Nate clung to her. They held each other so tightly, it was hard to tell. Marcus, on the other hand, stood next to me. As I flipped through pages of documents and notes, he looked over my shoulder. All of this, we'd put together in our unexpected time off between doing missed classwork and being on punishment. Fortunately, after my father saw the evidence and heard our speeches, he agreed to come as a chaperone to the hearing.

"Alissa," my father called, passing through the small crowd of demonstrators waving signs. He'd parked the car while we went on ahead to get a spot in the front. As I turned, I spotted him ducking a cleverly written sign being vigorously waved by one of the protestors.

"I didn't expect so many people," my father said when he finally approached. "You guys sure you don't want me to speak?" He looked between Marcus and me while giving Nate and Janice a quick glance. They kept silent, directing my father back to me.

I grinned. "C'mon, dad. We've got this."

"Just in case," my father said. "I'll be right behind you."

"Alright!" Marcus said, emphasizing his exclamation with a quick clap. "Let's do this."

Though I'd be doing all the talking, he said this like we were truly in this together, which we were. "Remember," I said to my friends. "We did this together!" I placed a hand before me, Marcus laid it on top of mine, and Nate and Janice joined in. We cheered.

When the doors opened, my father gave us some space, allowing us to enter on our own. As we did, a body pushed against me, followed by a familiar voice saying, "Excuse me."

I looked up and locked eyes with Principal Moss. A stunned expression flashed across his face and disappeared almost instantly as he eyed the three of us. He flashed us a toothy grin, "Well, look at the four of you. Marcus," he said as his expression softened. "How's your father?"

"He's... good," Marcus choked. "Ummm..."

Marcus' voice trailed off with a wide-eyed expression. My father had managed to get Mr. Kahale checked into a facility. Still, that information was only known to my immediate family, Marcus' family, and whoever they told. I couldn't imagine them telling Principal Moss.

The corners of Moss' lips turned upward. "Good. It's been hectic without Coach Kahale around. I wish him my best." With that, he turned on his heels and disappeared into the building.

The four of us seemed to share a collective stunned expression.

"What was that?" Nate gasped.

From behind us, my father called, "You four are holding up the line."

As we entered, I took Marcus' hand, giving it a gentle squeeze. "This'll work out," I said.

"I hope so," Marcus said.

With a forward jut of his chin, he pulled me onward to our seats, trying so hard to exhibit the confidence and enthusiasm of a leader. Nate and Janice followed behind. We'd all risked so much to clear his father's name. Between the hard work and our own personal and academic standings at the school, there was no way we'd give up now. We needed to clear Mr. Kahale's name and restore a sense of peace and healing in the Kahale family. On top of all that, we suspected someone of embezzling funds from the school account. We had a sense of suspects, but no motive, so all we could do is cast enough of a shadow of doubt over our audience to get them to dig deeper.

Taking our seats, I shuffled through the papers again. I ignored most of the conversations occurring in scattered groups around the room. However, I caught a few comments that pertained to the need to replace the entire school board and county council. Those types of comments, I thought, were extreme and likely spoken from a place of ignorance.

The rapid banging of a gavel brought everyone in the room to silence as an older woman, our school superintendent, stood, addressing us all.

"We gather today amidst a crisis," she began. "We are underfunded and understaffed. These last few months, we've hired independent auditors to do research and make recommendations. As a result, we've drafted a series of amendments upon which we intend to vote in our next meeting..."

As she continued with more of the same rhetoric, I became aware of how damp the papers I clutched in my hand had become. I set these papers and my notes on my lap, running my hands over them in an attempt to smooth out the crinkles. When I was done, I wiped my sweaty palms on my jeans.

To my left, Marcus eyed me with a half-cocked smile. Behind me, my father gave me a wink while Nate and Janice shot me a quick thumbs up. I returned the thumbs up, though I definitely didn't feel okay. Somewhere between our superintendent finishing her little introduction and my momentary lapse in attention, someone else had taken the podium. To the center, a screen displayed a slideshow from which this new person appeared to be literally reading from the presentation. I rolled my eyes, desperate for this boredom to end, and even more desperate for the release of this pang of anxiety creeping over me. Public speaking, though I could do it, was something I tried to avoid regularly. It shouldn't come as a surprise that I didn't immediately raise my hand when the floor was finally opened for questions and comments from the public.

In front of the room, a small squirrelly man held a microphone. He scurried on over to each person who happened to raise their hand. He didn't seem too discriminatory, either. The first man he handed the microphone to was elderly and dressed in sweatpants as though he decided to drop by after going to a fitness class. The elderly man took the microphone and spoke, "You say our kids are going to have to pay to play the sport. What about our kids from impoverished families? I know for a fact my grandkids wouldn't be able to play."

"Great question," our superintendent said. "Individual schools may set up scholarship funds through their boosters...."

On *boosters*, my heart seemed to skip a beat while Marcus perfunctorily nudged Janice and me while Nate shot me a sideways glance.

"...So, there's no reason your grandkids, or any of our students, wouldn't be able to play."

A few more questions were fielded. All of these were answered in similar unsatisfactory ways. Finally, when the gentlemen with the wireless microphone came to our side of the auditorium, my hand shot up. I was ready and almost snatched the microphone from the man when he handed it to me.

"I'm a student at Lenape High," I began. "And I don't believe any of this." I held up the papers we'd organized. "I have here our own research. The district has a lot of spending totally unaccounted for. Honestly, I'm surprised your independent auditors missed it." Though I heard a few gasps and murmurs, I continued to talk. "It's like, you've got a phantom school. The spending seems to be documented, but the numbers, something around ten million, don't add up."

A cacophony of conversations erupted, followed by the banging of the gavel. The squirrelly moderator attempted to take the microphone from me, but I pulled it away as Marcus, Nate and Janice seemed to form a barrier around me. The pounding of the gavel and the murmur of the crowd seemed to only increase in volume.

"Now, listen," our school superintendent began, attempting to hush the crowd. With a tight expression on the superintendent's face, she said, "I don't know who you are but —"

"I'm not finished," I said, silencing her and myself at the same time. I cleared my throat. "A lot of the money seems to be coming from Lenape High —"

My microphone cut off suddenly, though that didn't keep me from shouting above the crowd. "Someone's robbing us of our opportunities to compete."

As the murmurs died down, somewhere in the room, I heard the pounding of feet up a flight of steps followed by the slamming of the rear door. The gavel banged again, and I realized someone had already taken the microphone from my hand.

"Young lady," our school superintendent said. "These are incredible allegations. What evidence do you have?"

"Spreadsheets, copies of receipts, some of which seemed to have been falsified, especially when compared to their copies," I said, holding up the evidence. "You can have these."

The squirrelly moderator reached out his hand with hesitation. I rolled my eyes and handed the papers over.

"So, you know," I said, directing my comment to both the superintendent and the moderator, "We made backups."

"Of course," the superintendent said when she'd received the papers, giving them the quick flip-through. "Impressive work. What did you say your name is?"

"Alissa Claude, I'm a junior. And these are my friends —"

Someone in the room cut me off with a shout. "Are you seriously going to consider the evidence of some kids?"

"She's one of mine," a familiar voice responded from the stage. Somewhere in the third row of what I took to be members of the board, Principal Moss stood, surprising me. My heart sank as the room grew silent again. He turned to the superintendent, "I'd seriously consider everything she's brought to the table."

Without further commentary, the meeting was adjourned. In a sudden onslaught of questioning glaring eyes and murmuring mouths, Marcus, Janice, Nate, and my father ushered me out into the street.

Chapter Thirty

Marcus

The central office building seemed to vomit us out into the streets where our eyes and ears met a sea of red shirts cheering us on. My heart raced with excitement as I glanced at Alissa.

She erupted with nervous laughter while Mr. Claude wrapped an arm around her shoulder, giving her a squeeze. "I'm so proud of you," he said. Making eye contact with each of us, he smiled. "All of us, I mean. Nice work."

"Thanks, Mr. Claude," I said, offering him my hand. Instead, he released Alissa and pulled me into a tight embrace.

"We're beyond that, son," he said.

When he released me, he turned to Nate and Janice, offering them a similar gesture. I, on the other hand, turned away as I felt the heat of tears forming in my eyes.

Alissa placed a hand on my shoulder. "Are you okay?"

Sniffing, I shook my head. "I'm just not sure we brought enough out for Dad's name to be cleared."

"I get it," she said, biting her lower lip. "But we did our best."

"Alright, everybody," Mr. Claude said. "Let's roll."

As he led us through the crowd, people seemed to part before him. For a brief moment, I imagined this must've been what it was like to be a celebrity. Catching a quick glimpse of Alissa by my side, I saw she didn't feel the same way. I took her hand. Together, we walked through the crowd.

People called out to us. "How'd you get your research?"

"No comment," Nate called enthusiastically.

"What exactly did you find?" Someone right next to us said as he reached out to me.

Janice pushed him away. "You need to back off."

I locked eyes with the man and shrugged. "Sorry... we've had a long few days."

With a tight-lipped smile and a nod, the man backed away.

Ignoring the other comments, Alissa and I passed through the crowd. Meanwhile, our own little PR team in the form of Janice and Nate responded with snappy remarks that failed to satisfy anyone's questions.

Up ahead, Mr. Claude's voice boomed, "Out of my way." Using only his size and weight, he pushed through a group of people itching to talk to us. Meanwhile, Janice and Nate continued to push at us from behind while I caught a glimpse of a sign that read, *WE DON'T WANT NONE UNLESS YOU GOT FUNDS HUN.*

Maybe they didn't want excuses, I mused, as we finally stepped through the crowd.

We stood in a clearing in the middle of the street. Behind us, the crowd still chanted. To our left and right, orange rubber traffic cones blocked off the road. A few officers stood about, watching the crowd. One caught my attention. When he waved, I recognized him as Officer Robinson. I waved back and faced our final obstacle.

We faced a line of news station vans parked alongside the sidewalk. Reporters busy with their commentary faced cameras. One reporter, a middle-aged woman, dressed in a pants suit, caught a glimpse of us. As she made a beeline toward us, Mr. Claude moved to block her path.

"Excuse me," she said, speaking to Mr. Claude.

"Can I help you?" He asked, crossing his thick arms across his barrel-shaped chest.

The reporter offered her hand, which Mr. Claude took, as she said, "I'm investigative reporter Shannon Doyle with WXMR-TV." She cleared her throat when Mr. Claude didn't respond in kind. Ms. Doyle continued. "Are these the kids who presented their research into the missing funds?"

Alissa stepped forward. "We are," she said. Rolling her eyes at Mr. Claude, she offered her hand. "I'm Alissa Claude. Don't mind my father."

"You've got five minutes," Mr. Claude said, taking a step back and pulling out his cell phone.

"Thanks, Dad," Alissa said. Turning to Ms. Doyle, she said, "And these are my friends."

While I stepped forward to shake the reporter's hand, I couldn't help but notice Janice turned to Nate as she fussed with her hair.

"And this is Janice and Nate," Alissa said.

Blushing, Janice turned, extended her hand, and quickly said, "Nice to meet you. I watch your show all the time."

"Is that so," Ms. Doyle said with a smile.

"We watch it together," Nate said.

Ms. Doyle chuckled. "It's a pleasure to meet all of you. What you did in there was incredible!" Speaking more to Mr. Claude than to us, she said, "Do you mind if I do a segment with you for tonight's broadcast?"

"You have my permission if Alissa agrees," he said. "The others will have to check with —"

"I'm good," Janice squeaked, holding up her phone. "My mom said it's okay."

Nate mumbled. "Same." Though, I never saw him actually check in with his parents.

With all eyes on me, I said, "Give me a second."

As I pulled out my phone, I heard shouting and screeching of tires. I looked up. People parted and pushed each other out of the way as a faded blue Honda plowed through the traffic cones. An officer stepped in front of the vehicle, blowing his whistle. As the vehicle picked up speed, the officer dove out of the way. The Honda gunned for us. I turned to see Alissa, wide-eyed and frozen in place.

"Look out!" I shouted as I ran toward her while the others got out of the way. I pulled her toward the news van. The car whizzed by, inches from where we stood moments ago. Screams and a resounding crash immediately followed.

Nose to nose, Alissa and I were pressed against each other, breathing heavily. I held my breath, losing myself in the depth of her dark brown eyes.

"Are you okay?" she said, her eyes searching my own.

"Yeah, I think so."

Somehow, my lips found hers. While sirens blared behind us, I lost myself in Alissa: her scent of coconut and vanilla, her lips warm and passionate, and her body against mine. My heart rate rose, and heat radiated between us until we pulled apart.

Panting, she said, "That was..."

Behind us, Janice and Nate cheered while Mr. Claude said with laughter in his voice, "Alright, you two, that's enough."

Alissa and I stepped apart, nervously glancing at the others, then each other. We both let out a laugh and followed our friends and her father back out to the road and away from our little cubby between the news vans.

* * *

Emergency lights from police vehicles and two ambulances flashed blue and red. Officers roped off a clearing with police tape. At the same time, paramedics busied themselves, helping someone out of the old Honda, now a crumbled wreck against the wall of the school district offices. Officer Robinson stood by, overseeing the process.

"That's the car I told you about," Nate called out to Officer Robinson.

Officer Robinson gave a quick glance, nodded, then turned back to overseeing the work at hand.

"Let go of me," a man shouted. Instead of heeding to his demand, the paramedics helped him up and lead him to the ambulance, where they sat him down, checking his vitals.

Beside me, Alissa gasped, as Janice said, "What're they doing with Mr. Walter."

"I have no clue," I said. I scratched my head. As a group, we had our vice principal, Mrs. Johnson involved. I had not suspected the school's head custodian.

Nate turned to me. "Bro. He was helping them that night with the boxes, remember?"

"Yeah," I said, looking around. "Where's Johnson and Moss though?"

That question hung in the air between the five of us, Mr. Claude included. As if answering our question, Principal Moss pushed his way down the steps and through the crowd until he was at the police line.

"Officers," Moss called. "Make sure you arrest that man, Walter Prior."

"We intend to," Officer Robinson responded. "If you didn't notice all the damage."

Moss' face flushed. "Yes, but there's more," he said, pulling something out of his pocket. "There's this." When Officer Robinson came over, Moss said, "Somehow, he and my vice principal, Loretta Johnson, have been working some backdoor deal. Right under my nose."

It's all their fault!" shouted Mr. Walter from the ambulance. He glared at us. "We would've gotten away with it if it weren't for those meddling kids!"

Officer Robinson turned, closing the distance between himself and Mr. Walter. "Sir, whatever you say and do can be used against you in a court of law. Now, let's finish up here, and there'll be plenty of time for us to talk down at the station."

Off in the distance, just beyond the ambulance, the police cruisers, and the cones, I caught a glimpse of a white BMW. In the meeting, when Alissa had paused, I recalled hearing someone charging up the steps and out the backdoor.

"She's getting away," I called, pointing to Johnson's car as it slowly backed out of a parking lot. She gunned the gas, causing her wheels to squeal, and sped away. Tapping the radio on his shoulder, Officer Robinson spoke a command. Sirens wailed, guaranteeing the capture of Mrs. Johnson. What she and Mr. Walter had done, I didn't know. Not precisely, anyway.

Ms. Doyle approached us, a camera following right behind her. "Wow! So, this will definitely be quite a story. I'm thinking," she held up her hands, visualizing the headline, "High School Heist: Local Teens Uncover Money Laundering Scam."

Within crossed arms and a raised eyebrow, Alissa stared at her. "Money laundering?"

"Well, yes," Ms. Doyle said, her enthusiasm deflated. "It's a— "

Janice squealed. "Don't mind her. Will we be on the front page?"

Ms. Doyle locked her attention on Janice, matching her enthusiasm. "You betcha!"

"Oh! My..." Janice said, holding her forehead. "I Need to..." Janice lost her balance, fainting into Nate's waiting arms.

In one quick stride, Mr. Claude closed the distance between himself and Nate. "Let's get her to an ambulance. "Ms. Doyle. If Alissa and Marcus are up for an interview, go ahead."

Ms. Doyle pulled out a notepad and scribbled something on it. "So, I guess you don't like my headline?"

Alissa shrugged. "If that's the story, we really don't know what's going on."

"We can only tell you what we found," I added. "You'll have to figure out why and how the loss of funds occurred."

"Fair enough," Ms. Doyle said. "Shall we?"

Hand-in-hand, Alissa and I followed her over to the news van, the camera trained on us the entire time. As Ms. Doyle asked her first question, relief flooded over me. Though I didn't know what Mr. Walter or Ms. Johnson were getting on about, or who else was involved, I had a feeling it would help to exonerate Dad. In time, I hoped he'd be able to get back to work, but he still had to deal with his alcoholism. According to his long-time friend and Alissa's father, Mr. Claude, it wasn't the first time he'd fallen so low.

By my side, Alissa chatted with enthusiasm. I grinned, loving the way her espresso brown skin and dimpled cheeks seemed to glow with vibrancy. Around us, the crowd of demonstrators still mingled about, having their private conversations, while occasionally glancing our way. Over by the ambulance, Nate stood protectively over Janice, who seemed to be recovering. By their side, Mr. Claude talked on the phone. We'd done it, my friends and I, and I didn't want this moment to end.

"Marcus!" Alissa said, her voice pulling me from my thoughts. "Ms. Doyle asked you a question."

Ms. Doyle chuckled. "It's okay, Marcus. Can you tell me about how this all began?"

Ignoring the camera trained on us, I started from the beginning: the shed broken into, the stolen boxes, the mysterious way in which Dad stopped going to work... everything.

As I told my story, I couldn't help catching Alissa out of the corner of my eye. She gazed at me warmly. With Alissa by my side, I felt like I could do just about anything. Nate and Janice, now making their way toward us, completed the team. I wouldn't have it any other way.

Chapter Thirty-One

Marcus

I don't know how many times my head nodded to the drone of my English teacher's lecture on *The Crucible*. But I jerked awake when the intercom bell sounded. Something like half the class, plus my teacher, seemed to look at me as they listened to the announcement.

Marcus

At this time, all students should report to the auditorium for our scheduled assembly.

I suppressed a groan. I'd rather experience the Salem Witch Trials as a witch than go to one of Principal Moss' assemblies.

After Ms. Johnson's and Mr. Walter's arrest, another assistant principal, plus our school secretary, Mrs. Heinemann, were arrested on several accounts of fraud. Somehow, they managed to siphon several hundred thousand dollars in funds from various places over the past twelve years. All this because Mr. Walter had evidently walked in on them while they were fudging test scores way back before everything went electronic. He threatened to tell. They offered him money to keep him quiet. Apparently, all of them had gotten greedy.

On top of that, they did all this under Moss' watch, without him knowing. Personally, I found it hard to believe Moss didn't know. Somehow, though, he got off scot-free.

As I shouldered my way through the crowd, I was suddenly flanked by Nate, Janice, and Alissa.

Janice was the first to speak. "Why is Mr. Dunbar still here." She groaned.

I laughed. "Get used to it."

Alissa shot me a knowing glance.

"Alissa," Janice whined. "What are you not telling me?"

"I guess you'll have to find out at the assembly like everyone else," Alissa sang.

"Fine!" Janice said.

Over the last several months, we'd had our share of administrators. Dunbar stayed on as Dad's long-term sub while he recovered. Dunbar was questioned by the police. Magically, he was able to produce the missing forty-six-hundred dollars. He claimed it had been at the bottom of the safe in the athletic office all this time. Though the story seemed thin, at best, they cleared him as a suspect.

In the meantime, Dad had been exonerated. Not only that, but he'd been offered a position at Lenape High as its permanent Assistant Principal because of his unmatched school record. Although his professional record seemed flawless, I still worried about his personal record because of his struggle with alcoholism. Adjusting to those findings would take me some time. Still, he was clean now, so I was glad to have him, along with my whole family back.

Rounding the next corner, we saw the lobby thinning out as the last of the students entered the auditorium. Principal Moss greeted some of the students as they passed him.

Spotting us, Moss called, "Alright, you four. Come on in here."

Despite our continued suspicions of him, we decided to let our search rest. After everything, he conveniently forgot about our suspension, showing us that no such record existed in his database.

Entering the auditorium, I spotted Dad on stage, dressed like an administrator: suit and tie.

"Bro," Nate claimed. "Is that the news? Your dad's gonna be one of our principals?"

"Yup," I said, grinning until my face hurt.

Taking our seats, I couldn't help but think about how proud I was to see my dad up there on that stage. I knew that the dark part of his life still existed within him. Hopefully, he'd never again have a relapse. But, if he did, I'd be there for him. Mine and Alissa's whole family would have his back.

Chapter Thirty-Two

Alissa

Once again, I found myself standing in the center of our team bus, leading a celebratory chant. With one game away from qualifying for the playoff, we managed to lead our division, losing only one of our games. All this, despite not having new uniforms. As of yesterday, that had changed.

As the bus pulled to a stop at Lenape High, Coach Becky stood.

"You all look so great in your new uniforms," she said.

We cheered, thankful that Mr. Kahale had come through for us upon his return to work. Still, I couldn't help but scratch the back of my neck for what seemed like the hundredth time. Despite having new uniforms, the tags itched. I hoped that would go away after several more washings. If not, I'd have to "accidentally" lose the tag and claim it had fallen right off.

After giving her usual speeches about MVPs, Coach Becky dismissed us. Halfway to my car, I heard Janice's familiar call.

She ran toward me, grinning. "We totally rocked rehearsal."

"Yeah!" I said. "I can't wait to hear you sing *When You're Home* next week."

With the discovery of the missing money, came a sudden release of all sorts of financial restrictions in the school, including the drama program. *In the Heights* had been approved and paid for. I couldn't be any happier for Janice to get to play her dream role as Nina.

"There's something else," Janice said, whipping out her phone and shoving it into my face. "Look what Abby Jenkins said!"

I stared at a screenshot of Abby Jenkins posing in a Penamore College t-shirt. The caption read, *They said I couldn't do it. I don't even like school. Hi, haters. Look where I'm going.*

I pushed the phone away.

"Lis!" Janice whined. "Abby's only in one class with you. And that's our P.E. class. She's in several of my classes and some of Nate's classes."

From the track, I spotted Marcus jogging toward us with Nate in tow.

"Sorry we're late," Nate said. "We were scoping out the area. You know. Making sure no reporters were still hanging around."

Janice rolled her eyes. "Now that you're all here, we can talk. No way Abby Jenkins could make it into a prestigious school like Penamore. She does, like, less than zero work."

"So, what are you saying?" Marcus said.

Gasping, she squeaked out. "Guys, we've got another case!"

Nate mimicked her enthusiasm, shouting. "My girl Janice is saying we have a case!"

Alissa

Marcus and I gave each other a grin and a knowing nod. We'd see about letting them take the lead.

THE END

Acknowledgements

Special thanks to the following:

The wonderful community within Bel Air Creative Writers Society: Robert Broomall, Keith Hoskins, Lisa Janele, Alan Amrhine, Mark Taylor, Kim, Kane, Diane Foster, and Terry Emery. You've journeyed with me throughout the writing process. You guys are amazing!

Heather Carson, my first beta reader. Here's to many more pre-publishing experiences together!

Asha at Field Day Press. Your critique of my work continues to push me to develop the characters and the narrative presented to you in this story.

My students who inspire my writing every day. While there are far too many to name, my second-period film students during the 2020 school have been especially inspiring.

My parents, Richard and Kathie Baldwin. You are my biggest fans!

Indies United Publishing House. It is here my work has found a home.

Lastly, to all the anonymous readers who will cozy up to this book in the years to come. Your influence on writers, whether they be independent or small press, is the most impactful. Please, consider letting me know what you thought of this book by leaving me a review, reaching out to me by email, posting to a blog, or following me on your favorite social media platform.

About the Author

Tim grew up in Syracuse, New York. He currently resides in Maryland where he teaches English, Creative Writing, Film, and Theatre on the middle school level. At the insistence of his own students, he began writing seriously in 2014.

He credits his love for story to his mother, who spent countless hours reading to him and his siblings when they were growing up. Growing up, he devoured the literary words of C. S. Lewis, J. R. R. Tolkien, Piers Anthony, and many others. Mysteries, thrillers, and fantasies are among the genre he most frequently reads.

When he's not writing, he's reading, teaching, camping, or enjoying a live music concert.

Visit Tim on the Web

www.timothyrbaldwin.com
facebook.com/timothyrbaldwin
Twitter @timothyrbaldwin
Instagram @timothyrbaldwin